GAL WONDER

by Diane Lee Baron

Firebringer Press
Baltimore, Maryland

Published by:
Firebringer Press
6101 Hunt Club Road
Elkridge, MD 21085

ISBN: 978-0-9773851-9-5

February, 2017

Printed in the United States of America

Cover Art by Todd Brugmans

Cover and Interior Layout by Ethan Wilson

ACKNOWLEDGEMENTS

This novel is dedicated to my Maryland convention friends. Within that illustrious grouping, special thanks go to:

Howard Weinstein, author and friend, who gently nudged my writing along year after year and who insisted that a dog should be in the novel.

Steve Wilson, publisher of Firebringer Press and friend, for believing that I had actually written a novel.

Todd Brugmans, graphic artist, for creating the awesome cover art of this novel.

Kevin O'Brien, for gifting me with a huge Batmobile replica and the Batman DVDs.

June Swords, whose delightful pose in a photograph led to the idea for the cover.

The Eigen and Eng-Kohn families, for being my supportive forever friends.

All the convention dancing girls- Suzanne, Laura, Renee, Tori, Barb, Ana and Carla.

With a heartfelt thank-you to Adam West!

CHAPTER ONE

"No!" said Sara Goode. "I absolutely will *not* do it!"

Her friend Jen batted her eyes and said, teasingly, "But *look* at him."

Sara looked. "What about him?"

"He looks like Adam West." Jen held her gaze and looked expectant. When Sara didn't react, she said again, "*Adam. West.*"

"That's no reason for me to go and hit on him."

"That's every reason for you to go hit on him. And since when do we need an excuse to hit on a man in a bar?" Jen placed two fingers on the twenty-dollar bill between them and slid it toward Sara.

Sara snatched the bill, crumpled it, and tossed it at her friend. "Spend that on something worthwhile. Like another round of martinis." Sara drained the last swallow of her chocolate martini, downing the glass with a bang. "Damn, these are delicious! Where have they been all my life?" She knew she had said it too loudly. Jen and Char were both gazing in surprise. Dammit, though, she wanted to steer the conversation away from Adam West.

Adam. West.

"Whoa, girl," Jen said. "Pace yourself. You don't want to be hung over at work tomorrow." As secretary to the principal at May View Elementary, Jen ran the school office with dedicated efficiency and knew that the principal had a keen nose for overindulgence on the part of the staff.

"Yeah," agreed Char. "Teaching kindergartners on a Friday is rough enough. No one needs an extra handicap going in." Young, sweet Charlotte wanted the best for everyone. In her first year as an art teacher, she effortlessly dazzled her students and Principal Johnson with her California blonde looks and her eagerness to please.

"Hmmph," Sara replied. She sat back and surveyed the cozy bar that was their weekly hangout. She enjoyed sitting in Sparky's with the girls, having a few laughs and a refreshing drink on a sunny and only slightly cool day in May. A tantalizing whiff of spring came through the door every time a new patron entered, and its sweetness gave a promise of warmer days to come. The late sun slanted through the front windows of the Southside bar, old tunes piped through the ceiling speakers, and life was good in Pittsburgh. But then, unfortunately, Sara made visual contact with the trio of suited gentlemen across the room, including the one who looked like--*No! Don't even think it.* She quickly averted her eyes and sighed in dismay.

She said irritably, "Why must everything be a contest, Jen? Why can't you just live in the moment? I am perfectly content sitting here with my two besties. I don't need male company to make this experience complete. And, I might add, your cash incentive is kind of offensive."

"It's all about the fun. Don't you think it's fun to challenge yourself and see what happens?" Jen asked.

Sara narrowed eyes. "Like the time you tried to see how many malted milk balls you could fit in your mouth at one time?" Sara enjoyed reminding Jen of that one particularly humiliating result of one of her many challenges.

Char giggled, flashing her dimples, and said, "Yeah! And Sara called 911 because she thought you were dying."

Sara and Char devolved into quiet hysterics, their shoulders shaking at the memory of Jen trying to explain the sticky mess to annoyed paramedics.

Jen raised her head, assuming a haughty manner. "Go ahead and laugh, girls. At least I tried. Which is more than I can say for you and your love life, Sara Goode."

"Oh, please! I don't see how hitting on those guys is going to lead to a fine romance. For one thing, I'm too old for them. They're what, maybe forty? And I've got too much baggage from my divorce to even consider starting with a new guy. I don't want to go through all that 'getting to know you' stuff. Ugh."

"I'm not buying what you're selling," Jen said, and turned a hurt look on Char. "As for you, Blondie, if I recall, a certain milk ball incident got you a hunky new boyfriend."

Charlotte's eyes flashed indignantly. "Do not *even* call me 'Blondie!'" Charlotte would push hard against anyone who dared to put her in the blonde bimbo category.

But it was true. Char had snagged Mitchell, the hunk under discussion, a Pittsburgh firefighter, as a result of the milkball incident. While his new recruit had swabbed Jen clean, Mitchell and Charlotte had managed to exchange names, numbers and the very vital relationship statistic that they were both single.

Jen sighed. "Sorry, Char. I do not define you by your hair color."

Char started to say, "Thank you," but Jen interrupted her with, "Much." This prompted Char to scoop up a handful of nuts from the bowl on the table and pelt Jen with them.

Sara was happy that laughter followed this exchange. She was a peacemaker who disliked any disagreements among her friends. To steer conversation away from both Char's physical attributes and any aging actors who once wore tights on television, she asked Jen, "So what's new in the school office?"

Jen sat up straight and cleared her throat. "This week I busted a fourth-grader who was running a black market eraser and candy bar ring in the school parking lot." Her look of pride suggested that this coup had her on a days-long personal high.

Sara feigned solemnity. "May View Elementary School couldn't function without Agent Jennifer's staunch defense of peace and justice."

Char started to hum "God Bless America," but Sara quietly motioned her to stop. "Don't encourage her." Then, tapping her fingers in time to the music coming through the speakers, she said, "I know this song."

Jen snapped her fingers thoughtfully. "Daydream... Daydream..."

Sara scooped the win. "'I'm A Believer' by the Monkees!" She looked Jen straight in the face, and said, "Ha! I can't believe I beat you. I *never* beat you."

Jen shrugged, took a nut from the bowl between them, and stared at it intently. "I knew that." She popped the nut into her mouth. "I was just giving you guys a chance." She began to sing the tune, and Jen joined in, *"'I'm a believer, I couldn't leave her if I tried.'"*

Jen stopped there, but Sara continued the next verse in a soft soprano, *"'I thought love was more or less a given thing, seems the more I gave the less I got.'"* Then she stopped, too, thinking for a moment. "Ain't that the truth?" Her shoulder-length, honey-brown hair slipped forward as she cradled her head in her arms.

Charlotte draped her arm around Sara's shoulders. "Let's not go down that road. This is a girls' night out. Hey, remember the time Jen wanted to see which one us could get a guy to laugh in the lingerie store?"

Sara smiled at the thought of one of Jen's more memorable challenges, since the only men present were arm-in-arm with their girlfriends or wives. It wasn't as easy a task as it would have been at the hardware store. Men in lingerie stores tended to walk with blinders on, pretending that they saw nothing of the frill and lace that assaulted them at every turn.

"Char was a shoo-in with that long, straight, shiny-blonde hair and those size 38 double-D cups," Sara said. "All she had to do was hold a teeny, tiny pink satin bra in front of her chest and say 'Girls, do you think this will fit?'"

Char smiled demurely. "Yes, that was fun, I have to admit."

"You make an art smock covered in paint look like the latest runway fashion," Jen said, reflecting for a moment before asking, "Why don't we play 'pop stars of the sixties?'"

Charlotte and Sara gave exaggerated groans and settled back firmly against the comfy fake leather seat of the booth. Sara gave a signal to the bartender that they wanted another round of martinis.

Sensing that her friends had reached their limit with games, Jen said, "Okay, okay, no contests. But really, which sixties star have you always had a crush on? And it can't be somebody from a fake boy band like The Monkees." Jen looked pointedly at Sara.

"Spoilsport," Sara muttered as she reached to her empty glass and managed to inhale the last drop of chocolate martini.

Jen gave a shrug then said, "I have one."

Sara humored her. "Okay, go on, who was your 'fave' guy?"

"Bob Dylan," Jen said, dreamily.

"Who?" Charlotte asked, confusion etched on her angelic face.

"He was before your time, sweetie." Sara patted her hand.

"Well, of course he was before my time! I'm not familiar with any singers from the sixties. I wasn't even born then! And please don't patronize me." Charlotte pouted as she pulled her hand away from Sara's. She sulked for a few seconds before giving up self-pity in favor of a long slurp of her remaining drink.

"You know who I mean, Char. *Bob Dylan.* He was so cool, with his black leather jacket and that full head of kinky hair. He was a soulful folk singer." Jen described her favorite rebel singer in the hopes of jogging Charlotte's memory.

"Nope. Never heard of him,"

Sara didn't want to rock the boat by disagreeing with Jen, but, honestly, there were better candidates than some guy who sang political songs in a really awful, twangy voice, and played a harmonica every chance he got. But, she kept her opinion quiet for once. "Char? Isn't there anyone from maybe the seventies that you can recall?"

"Okay, I don't know if this guy is from the seventies because he's still here, but hands down, it would be Mick Jagger. I mean, I know he's ancient, but he is *so* hot. Mick could rock my world." Charlotte closed her eyes and dreamed of swollen lips and swaying, sexy hips.

"So you like the bad boys, too, huh?"

"So what *good boy* do you like?" asked Jen.

Sara knew that this conversation was moving dangerously close to a subject she wanted to avoid. More, it was a subject she suspected Jen was trying hard to dredge up, even though Jen had long ago made a solemn promise to leave it alone. She scoured her mind for a runner-up candidate from the Sixties. Anyone but Adam West.

"I guess it would have to be squeaky-clean Bobby Sherman. He was a cutie pie on the television show, *Here Come the Brides.*"

Jen broke into a rowdy chorus of "*'Julie, Julie, Julie, do you love me? Julie, Julie, Julie do you care?'*"

Char stared, open-mouthed. "Again, I don't know that song. And I don't really think I'm interested in hearing it. I admit I'm the baby of the group and don't get all your references, but I feel some things need to be left in the past. How bubblegum can you get?" Char tried not to choke on the handful of peanuts that she had been munching on.

Jen stopped in the middle of a particularly pitchy note. "Char, if you think the lyrics are lame, you should have heard Bobby Sherman's singing!" The bartender set down their fresh drinks on the table with his eyebrows furrowed in consternation, but it didn't look like he was going to shut them down. Yet.

"Okay, that's enough," Sara hissed, as the bartender walked away. "Bobby may not have been the greatest singer, or songwriter," she added, "but his music spoke to me." She tapped the area over her heart for effect.

"Oh, God," Jen said. She picked up her martini and held up the glass in mock salute. "We're pathetic. Our music idols are a rebel, a geriatric rocker and the king of bubblegum music. No wonder we're here and, might I add, all alone on a Thursday night."

Char said, "There's always those cute guys over there. They seem to be interested in us." She tossed off a flirty smile towards the young businessmen. She was dating Mitchell, but that didn't stop her from spending time with other attractive members of the opposite sex, on a friendly basis only, of course.

Sara gave a quiet sigh. Char was indeed the baby of the group in her mid-twenties, while Jen was sliding into her mid-thirties. Sara, well, she was on the wrong side of forty. Never mind that she'd always had a tendency to look younger than she actually was. She was thankful that her hair stylist did a fabulous job of keeping her roots covered and her highlights believably honey blonde. With her funky horn-rimmed glasses framing her brown eyes, Sara felt that she'd covered her bases, and her age, rather well. But not well enough to capture the interest of a very young investment banker or insurance writer, or whatever those guys across the room were likely to be.

As Jen and Char concocted a scheme to meet the only too-ready-and-willing men, Sara replayed her broken record of insecurities. Being a kindergarten teacher would keep her young for a while longer, she hoped. How many "women of a certain age" sat on the floor playing *Hungry, Hungry Hippos* on a regular basis? She could catch a kid jumping off a desk into midair without blinking an eye. But when would that all go away? When would she finally have to face the fact that she was getting older, and that her chances for happiness and love were turning to dust? She shook her head to clear the negative thoughts that burned deep tracks through her mind. She looked up and realized that Jen had just spoken to her.

"What?" Sara asked.

"Stand up, and come on! We're going over to introduce ourselves to those guys," Jen said. "We'll leave the Adam West guy for you." Jen picked up her martini glass and used it to indicate the men across the room.

Sara almost knocked over her drink. "No, wait! He doesn't look like Adam West. Okay, his jaw kinda reminds me of Adam's." She cradled her drink and spoke with urgent desperation. "I'm serious, I can't do this. I'm too old for those guys."

Char hooked her arm around Sara's elbow and pulled her gently out of the booth. "Doesn't matter. We're going, and you're coming with us."

The girls walked over to the booth filled with prospective bachelors, Sara lingering behind her friends. Jen and Char smiled and introduced themselves while the men nodded eagerly. Jen and Char slipped into the booth and quickly paired off with two sandy-haired men in finely cut suits and Hugo Boss ties. The leftover guy, the one with the sculpted chin but definitely myopic eyes, looked up at Sara and shrugged his shoulders.

"I guess that makes us buddies," he said.

She edged away. "I guess." Sara couldn't see the resemblance to Adam West at all now. In fact, if she shut one eye and cocked her head in a certain way, this guy looked startlingly like Mr. Magoo. But then, she was a decade or so older than he was, so she had nothing over him.

"I'm Tim. Tim Jones." The guy reached out his hand, and Sara reluctantly extended hers for a brief shake. "I'm Sara," she mumbled. "Sara Goode."

"Nice to meet ya, Sara. I once met a girl named Sara. At a Steelers' game downtown. Maybe you know her? Sara Dubinsky?"

"Oh sure, we Saras all know each other. There's a newsletter."

"Oh, awesome!" enthused Tim, looking past Sara. "Here come the flaming cocktails!" The waiter had, in fact, arrived with a tray of drinks, drinks which, moments later, were on fire. Sara's attempt at humor had been missed.

Sara took an awkward step backward in surprise, slightly turning her ankle, and grabbing on to the nearest table ledge. As she did so, she bumped Tim's elbow and some of his drink dripped on to his tie. Before she had time to think, Tim's tie went up in flames. His glass crashed to the concrete floor as he began slapping his chest. The fire licked his face as his eyes grew huge in fear. Sara heard someone scream. A swift-thinking buddy grabbed a jacket from the booth and smothered both Tim and the flaming tie, effectively snuffing out the fire and probably suffocating Tim at the same time.

"Wow," was all Sara could manage amidst her shock and dismay.

Tim's buddies pulled him into the men's room. Sara remained frozen.

"Now that's something you don't see every day," Char said breathlessly.

Jen grabbed Sara's arm and guided her back to their booth, where they silently put on their coats and gathered their belongings.

"Let's get out of here before they press charges," Jen murmured.

As they ran to keep up with Jen, Sara leaned into Char and whispered, "I didn't mean to set him on fire."

Char patted her arm. "I know, honey."

The shock lifting, Sara stopped in her tracks and demanded, "You see? This is the shit that happens to me. *All the time*. I try to be nice to a man, and I accidentally set him on fire."

Jen reached back, grabbed Sara, and pulled her along toward the parking lot.

"Sara?" Char said quietly.

"Yeah?"

"That guy didn't really look like Adam West."

No, Sara said to herself, *there's only one Adam West. And I'll never come within ten miles of him.*

Char went on, "Adam West is much better looking, even if he is an older dude. I know because Mitchell and I watched that second Batman movie last week."

Sara's eyes narrowed. "What movie are you talking about? There was only one made after the first season of *Batman.* Oh, God, I have a stitch in my side." She grabbed her right side and began vigorously massaging her muscles.

"Not true. There's another movie. It was a hoot. You should watch it since you have a crush on Adam West and all," Char said.

"See you both tomorrow!" barked Jen. They had reached their cars. Jen was in her car, revving the engine and, before Sara had even found her keys, had peeled out of the parking lot.

"Geez. You'd think we set somebody on fire or something," said Sara as she struggled to free her keys from the tangle of her iPod headphones.

"Well, yeah. You sort of did, Sara," said Char as she placed her key into her door lock. "Listen, I'll bring the movie to school tomorrow."

"Okay," said Sara, breathing heavily and beeping open the electronic lock on her Mini Cooper. "Well, bye." She never once considered that things could get any weirder in her life than what they were at that moment.

She had had too much to drink. She had let Jen talk her into going outside her comfort zone. She certainly wasn't proud of the fact that she had set a man on fire. She hoped that the 'Burning Man' incident was never spoken of again, though, knowing her friends and family, it would.

And yet, only one thought dominated her attention right now. She muttered it out loud as she looked at her own eyes in the rear view mirror:

"That guy looked *nothing* like Adam West!"

CHAPTER TWO

"What… the… hell?" Sara was a Macy's Thanksgiving Day balloon that had just been punctured by a peashooter. She was one of those giant helium balloons like Underdog or Popeye that floated down the New York streets, tethered to the hands of clowns. Except all the air was slowly hissing out of her belly, and a chin dive into the pavement was imminent.

All she'd had to drink this evening was hot chamomile tea with a wedge of lemon, so there was no sane explanation for the hallucinations.

"Why do I feel so disoriented?" she asked. "And how did I not know that there was a second Batman movie? I have been all about the Bat since the show aired. I tell everyone I'm this huge Adam West Batman fan, and yet I didn't even know this movie existed. I find that strange, don't you, Joe?"

Her friend Joe Norris sat across the room from her, watching her big brown eyes plead for some kind of rational answer to her question. Joe thoughtfully placed his root beer on an end table, got up from the recliner and crossed to Sara on the couch. It was evident from his tight jaw and raised right eyebrow that Joe wasn't up for any drama-queen nonsense. "What's the big deal? So you missed a movie from 2003! I'm pretty sure it didn't break any box office records, if it even made it to first-run theaters."

Sara slumped on the couch, hugging the squishy cupcake pillow Charlotte had given her last Christmas. She peeked up at Joe, casually pretentious with his spiky blonde hair, pale skin and L.L. Bean cargo pants with matching polo shirt.

"I don't understand how it's possible for me to be such a huge geeky Batman fan without knowing about this movie." Sara bit the edge of her pillow. "But that's actually not the worst of it."

"Oh? Go on."

"Joe... Adam West got *old*." She cringed as she said the words, "I mean, *way* older."

"As have we all."

"Yes, but my school-girl crush was on a man who was in his early forties, not someone who's over eighty. God, I'll bet he has an AARP card! In my mind, I kind of froze Adam West at the age he was when he was the Caped Crusader. I just never considered that he had become," she lowered her voice to a whisper, "a senior citizen."

"Get over it, Sara. It's a non-issue. The fact that you lost track of some sixties pop icon for a few years doesn't amount to a hill of beans. Adjust your mental picture of him and move on."

"You don't understand, Joe! Seeing him so...*ancient*... it makes me wonder what the hell was I doing all these years. Forty years have gone by and what have I done with myself?"

Joe rolled his eyes, then said, "Okay, let's see. After graduating from high school here in Pittsburgh, you went to the University of Connecticut. Why Connecticut? We don't know, but let's continue. After that you moved to New York City, got your master's degree and became a teacher. And, oh yes, you married some bozo who turned out to be a raving lunatic. Fortunately, you divorced the bozo and returned home a year ago to make a new start, for which your family and friends are quite thankful. " Joe nodded, satisfied. "That covers a good thirty years, give or take a decade," Joe said with a smirk.

"Aaargh!" Sara buried her face in the pillow. "You just proved my point. I've led a boring and bungled life. Go away and let me wallow in my discontent." She rubbed her stomach and pouted.

"And I don't feel so good."

"Are you sure it wasn't the second helping of popcorn with extra butter? That'll gum up the works."

Sara held the pillow up against her stomach and groaned. "Maybe. I don't know. But the movie didn't do me any favors either. I need a moment to try and figure this out."

Joe sighed and returned to the recliner. "I'm not sure if I understand how seeing an older Adam West has caused this middle-age meltdown, Sara. But I'll just sit over here quietly while you figure it out." He closed his eyes and leaned back his head. "I'll think about the cutie I met at the Gap last night."

Sara took a deep breath and released it in a long, drawn-out exhale. The insanity had started when Charlotte had loaned her Mitchell's copy of *Return to the Batcave* in the teachers' lunchroom yesterday. Char had produced the box in full view of the lower elementary staff, causing Sara to panic, snap it out of Char's hand and hide it in her lesson plan book. She hadn't wanted anybody asking about it, as her teenage interest in Batman and his superhero trappings had always seemed slightly illicit. There was that "utility belt" and all.

She would reflect on those guilty feelings later, she had promised herself. Upon receipt of the DVD, she was entirely focused on getting it home and viewing it. Watching her teen idol alone seemed so pathetic, however, that she invited Joe for a movie night. He enjoyed pop culture, although his interests leaned more toward the movies while she favored the old TV shows.

Now, however, Sara was beginning to think that her nostalgic trip to the past should have been made alone. She wanted to mull over her anxious thoughts at seeing her idol in his declining years. She felt like she owed an apology to someone—Adam West—she guessed, for losing sight of what used to be her prime focus—her obsession.

Joe's eyes popped open, and he broke the silence. "You know, I really dug that movie. Especially when Adam West did the Batusi. Now that's one older dude who can still get down." Joe leapt from his chair and gyrated his hips, imitating the iconic dance, but suggesting a Pentecostal worshipper suffering from food poisoning. Sara could only stare.

He rambled on, "Nice twist—actors who used to be superheroes, trying to solve an actual crime. And the two guys who played Adam West and Burt Ward's younger selves were spot-on in their portrayals, don't you think?"

"Mmm-hmm." Sara was too busy chewing on her lower lip to answer. Joe didn't seem to really need a response to keep on with his monologue about the film.

"Do you think that stuff in the movie really happened, or was it a spoof? I couldn't tell. All that crazy stuff about Burt Ward really getting injured during the stunts and Adam getting caught with girls in his hotel room. It's hard to tell what was real and what was put in for laughs." Joe plopped back into the recliner. "Makes me wonder about those guys. It had to be nuts running around in tights and a cape and having all those chicks crushing on you."

Sara looked up now, annoyed. "*I* was one of those 'chicks.' When I was thirteen years old, Batman was the hottest thing I'd ever seen."

"I can relate. That's how I felt about *The Dukes of Hazzard*." Joe closed his eyes and smiled lewdly. "Daisy Duke in cut-offs, riding the General Lee? It changed the way I watched television."

"Would you like to be alone with your pervy fantasies?" asked Sara. "And you're such a baby. Daisy Duke…" She shook her head. "But you probably have an idea of what happened to her over the years." She gave a heart-felt sigh. "I loved Adam, and then I left him high and dry. I haven't thought about Batman or Adam West since junior high school. What kind of a fair-weather fan am I?"

With both hands, Joe slapped the arms of the recliner. "Honey, you went on to live your teen years. To date boys your own age and to experience your first kiss, to have fights with your parents, to get your nipples pierced. Oh, sorry, that was me. But the point is, Batman couldn't make that journey with you, Sara."

"Why not?"

"Because you got older and wanted *real* boys to play with. Sorry, but it's true: Adam West just played a character on a television show. As far as you're concerned, he was never *real*."

Joe spoke the words kindly, but Sara still stuck her tongue out at him. She sat up and threw the cupcake pillow at him, missing his head by inches.

"I know that, you big goof, I'm not delusional. I just feel bad that someone who meant the world to me could keep on living his life without me noticing. He's still a handsome dude, but he isn't the Adam West I remember. And that bugs me." She stood up, straightened her loose sweater and pulled down the creases in her jeans.

"Come on, Joe," she pleaded. "Tell me where the time went. And, for that matter, where did my collection of old movie star magazines with articles about Adam West go? I'll just bet my mom threw them out the minute after I left for college."

Joe got up and went to carefully check his appearance in the mirror on Sara's family room wall. He corrected a few errant hairs. "Nahhh, I'm sure Gertie has kept your movie star mags for the last few decades, sure in the motherly knowledge that one day you might ask for them." He blew himself a kiss in the mirror. "I mean, my mom has kept everything that belonged to me. And I do mean *everything*."

"You were a spoiled, only child. Mother Norris probably has a curl from your first haircut."

"The curl? She kept a trash bag full!"

Sara had met Joe's mother a few times, and she definitely wanted to keep her son tied to those old apron strings. No wonder he was backwards in his interactions with women.

"Gertie is such a neat freak," Sara complained about her own mother. "My old magazine clippings probably looked like trash to her. She was always dying to rid the house of my stuff."

"You've got it wrong, Sara. You're displacing your anger on poor ol' Gertie. But wait a sec—You've been so blasé about having friends who are all younger than you. I bet you don't even think about how much older you are than Char or Jen, or me even."

"I'm not that much older than the rest of you! Geez. I'm just saying that I'm trying to reconcile the past with the present. My whole life has been dedicated to moving forward, taking that next corner, climbing up that ladder."

"You gonna sing, Miss Andrews?"

Lacking the pillow to serve as a weapon, Sara just swatted Joe's shoulder. Then she sighed. "It's just that I've always believed in *carpe diem*."

"So seize the day!"

"But I've been living a lie. I've been so focused on what's ahead, I've forgotten to look back and remember the things that used to mean something to me. I'm always running full steam ahead, leaving behind friendships, burning up my memories of the past."

She stopped and poked a finger into his chest. "Don't you think that there are things from your past that have made you who you are today? Those things should be recognized and honored!"

"Okay, if you say so. What did Batman give you that's part of the Sara Goode that I know and love today, pray tell?" Joe moved away from the finger pushing into his sternum, grabbed his half-filled glass off of the coffee table and once again took possession of the overstuffed recliner.

Sara began to pace. "Well, let's see." A string of ideas was rapidly taking shape in her mind. "Batman gave me the template for my idea of the perfect man."

Joe choked on a mouthful of root beer. "Your perfect guy wears tights and a cape?"

"Um, no." Sara rolled her eyes. "That would be fun, but that's just a fantasy. I always felt that he should be tall and broad-shouldered, with a square jaw and green or blue eyes."

"You're not so picky on the eye color, then?" Joe teased.

"Nope. As long as the guy has long legs up to his armpits, the color of his eyes is negotiable."

Sara stopped in front of her fish bowl and began making fish faces at Goldie. The goldfish ignored her and quickly swam inside the underwater plaster castle. Goldie had been a gift from Sara's mom and had somehow had managed to live for over a year. Sara was fond of the little fish, because she was such a survivor.

"Ohhhh-kaaaay," Joe drawled out the word. "So Batman was your idea of male physical perfection. I'll just bet your teenage self wanted to spend some time hanging in that Batcave, mmmm?"

"I won't deny that I felt my first 'stirrings' around that time."
Sara felt herself blush. "But Batman always showed such respect
for women; it's like he put them on a pedestal. That's the way I've
always wanted guys to treat me." She shook a few flakes of fish food
into Goldie's bowl then resumed a circle of the room. "When I was
first dating, I thought that I should be treated like a princess. I'd give
out only a chaste kiss at the end of the evening."

"Holy convent, Batman!" Joe leaped to his feet and placed his
hands soundly on his hips. "No man could be a match for your frigid
lips!"

Sara laughed, both at Joe's boy wonder imitation and at her
clearly clueless girlhood.

She tapped her lips with her pointer finger. "You know, Johnny
looks a bit like Bruce Wayne, I mean, Adam West." She made the
comment absently, thinking aloud. As soon as the words had passed
her lips, Sara realized that she shouldn't have said them. She was
stupidly venturing into combat territory without an adequate arsenal
of weapons.

Joe immediately opened fire with the anticipated volley. "So
you've told me before. Why is it, then, that you can't seem to give
poor Johnny the attention he deserves? He fits your ideal to a tee,
and yet you treat him like a second-class citizen."

Joe became animated as he went on, "I mean, I like Johnny. I like
hanging out with him on Saturday nights. You wouldn't think that a
manly carpenter like Johnny and a pretty-boy IT guy like me--"

"You're not that pretty."

"—*Would get along*," Joe finished forcefully, acknowledging her
obligatory insult only with the withering glare it deserved. "It just
goes to show you that anything is possible. If I wasn't hetero, I'd
have little man crush on Johnny."

Joe was a loyal, although opinionated, friend, but Sara wished
he would focus on his own dating issues and forget about her non-
relationship with Johnny. Joe seemed to be always awaiting his
perfect match, which was a shame since he might be having some
fun until his dream girl arrived.

Now, Johnny Nash, with his trim, six- three frame, sky-blue eyes and sandy, heading-to-salt-and-pepper hair was definitely a manly man. When Sara stood next to Johnny, her five foot six inches felt petite, even though she was more rounded out, with curves where there should be curves and some bumps where there shouldn't be bumps. She'd always liked men who made a strong statement with their appearance. She worked on the premise that if a man couldn't wear a cape and a cowl on a regular basis, then he'd better be built solid, and a bit of girth was not a problem.

Also, Johnny, unlike Joe, had no fear of the opposite sex.

"Joe, I'm seeing Johnny for lunch tomorrow, so kindly stuff it."

"Thank goodness for that, even if it is just throwing the dog a bone." Joe snorted and looked away, pretending to pick an invisible loose thread from the fabric of his shirt. "If I'm not mistaken, Johnny adores you and would gladly keep you on a pedestal for as long as your princess behind would care to sit on it."

Sara laughed. "That sounds dirty, Joe."

He was still miffed, but the corner of his mouth twitched in amusement. "If the glass slipper fits, Cinderella…"

"Enough! We were talking about Batman, and I'd like to get back to that." Sara was relieved to turn the conversation away from her old, ambivalent feelings about Johnny and toward her new, ambivalent feelings about Adam West and his golden age.

"I'm going to go out on a limb here, Sara. I have a theory. But first you have to promise me that your lethal finger," Joe gently rubbed his chest where she had just poked him, "and any other dangerous body parts will not make contact with me if you don't like what I have to say."

Sara thought of all sorts of saucy body part comments she could make, but decided not to give Joe any ideas. He was a sweetie, but Joe was definitely too… *Joe*… to be her type. "Come on, Joe. Just spit it out."

"Huh-uh. Promise me."

Sara sighed deeply. She sometimes forgot that Joe could be a real pain. "Okay, I promise."

"Sara, I think... Hmm, how should I say this? Okay, here it is: I think that your issue isn't about Batman—it's about how you don't want to get any older." Joe covered his head with his hands. "Please don't hurt me."

"God, you are such a wuss, Joe." Sara picked up a crystal mermaid, a relic of a recent, all-gal trip to the Virgin Islands. "Didn't we just go over this age thing?"

"Well, not exactly. We talked about how you've lost some time through the process of aging, but we didn't discuss how that makes you feel."

"Ugh. *Feelings*." Sara ran her fingers over the smooth crystal fins of the mermaid. "Okay, I do feel a bit scared about being squarely in middle-age, and maybe seeing one of my icons as a senior citizen has set off the alarms. I'll never see thirty, let alone sixteen, again. But, I think I look pretty darn good, and, heaven knows, I feel like I'm half my age most of the time. So let's just let this age thing go."

Joe said nothing. After a moment, and with sudden determination, she announced, "You know what? I want to tell him."

Joe shrugged. "Okay." He took another drink. "Wait, tell who?"

"Adam West."

"Gotcha." He took another drink. "Tell him what?"

Good question. "I—Everything! I want to give an acknowledgement. To let Mr. West know that he touched my life. That the spirit of his character has stayed with me from my teen years until my—until now."

"That's just weird, Sara."

"Shut up and drink your pop."

"Root beer. Don't call it 'pop.' It's so... *Pennsylvania*."

"*I'm* so Pennsylvania. And my idea isn't weird." She frowned. "Is it?" At his silence, she admitted, "I suppose it could be seen as a bit wacky."

Joe stood up and walked over to her. He took the crystal mermaid out of her hands and placed it carefully back on the shelf. Then he grasped Sara's shoulders and said, "No, I guess it's not all that weird. You always have been an original, Sara. Do what you need to do, and write to Adam West. But know I'll be here for you if you start feeling a middle-age crisis coming on. I happen to think you are spectacular at whatever age you are."

Sara smiled. "Thanks, Joe. I appreciate that."

Joe released her and went to the kitchen to root around for food, as he always did. "So how are you going to do it? How are you going to thank Adam West?" He opened the refrigerator door and began to review bottles and Tupperware containers. "More importantly, do you have any cheese?"

"On the second shelf, in the back, by the margarine." She watched Joe extract a block of cheddar, sniff it, then noisily search for a knife in the silverware drawer. "Honestly, Joe? I'm not sure what I'll do about Adam West. But I'm definitely going to...do something."

He winked at her and said around a too-generous slice of cheddar. "You go, Gal Wonder!"

She heard a soft knock on her front door.

"I think someone is at front door," she said.

"Well, go and answer it," said Joe, who returned with another huge wedge of cheese in his hand.

She looked suspiciously toward the entry hall. "It's late," she said. "It's after ten o'clock."

"Ask who it is, silly. Burglars don't knock on the front door."

"Who's there?" Sara said in a raised voice.

"Sara, it's me, Char. Open the door, please. It's an emergency."

Sara rushed for the door and yanked it open. It banged on the wall. Outisde stood a disheveled Char, carrying a small, golden-haired dog under one arm and a large bag under the other. Char hustled past Sara into the house and dropped the bag to the floor. Cradling the dog in her arms, she said, "You have to help me Sara. You're my only hope."

CHAPTER THREE

"So what happened next?" Johnny asked. "I didn't know Char had a dog."

"She just got it yesterday." Sara was telling the story to Johnny Nash on their lunch date at SouthSide Works. The new shopping district was really hopping after the renovations that replaced steel mills with quaint shops and chain restaurants.

"Apparently, he's a shelter mutt—a birthday gift for Mitchell. Only the whole thing backfired when Mitchell had an allergy attack the minute the poor puppy jumped in his lap."

"Who buys someone a pet without finding out if they are allergic first?" Johnny said. "No wait, don't answer that. *Char* does."

"She does indeed. And here's the kicker. Mitchell told Char that either he or the dog would have to go. I guess he's so allergic that having a dog is a deal-breaker."

"Fortunately she didn't have time to get too attached to the dog. Is she going to take it back to the shelter?"

"No. She refuses. They'd put it to sleep, and Char could never do that to an animal. So she can't keep the dog at her place because of Mitchell. Jen can't have dogs in her apartment. Joe absolutely refuses to have a dog because of his pristine furnishings. And all of Char's family live in the Midwest."

"Which leaves you," Johnny said with a twinkling smile. "And what was in the big bag that Char carried into your place?"

Sara slumped forward on the table, burrowing her head in her arms. "Dog food. And now I have dog food and a goofy-looking mixed breed."

"You're not particularly fond of animals, if I recall correctly."

"I'm ambivalent," Sara said. "And yet, here I am, with a dog waiting for me in my house, no doubt drooling on the furniture and digging holes in the carpet."

"You have a soft heart, Sara Goode," Johnny said.

"More like rocks in my head. I'm only keeping the dog until Char can find him a permanent home. She thinks it won't take too long. I guess I'll survive, but I can't guarantee the dog will make it." She moved back from the table as their waitress delivered cheesecake—key lime for her and chocolate for Johnny. Her mouth watered. "Yum."

As Sara attacked hers, Johnny said, "I talked to Joe yesterday. He mentioned something about Adam West. You two were going to watch a Batman movie together?"

"Joe is such a gossip. He's like Joan Rivers and Geraldo Rivera rolled up into one. Well, here's the scoop: Yes, we watched the movie and yes, I'm going to write Adam West a letter."

"A letter? Sure, why not?" Johnny stopped his chocolate cheesecake-laden fork halfway to his mouth. "It's not like you're stalking the guy, right?' He winked at Sara as the cheesecake made its way through his full lips and into his mouth. "Oh, sweet heaven, this is good. Want to try some?"

Sara was distracted by his obvious sensual delight in the cheesecake. He rolled the smooth creamy texture around his tongue, sucking every last morsel of chocolate sweetness out of the forkful. Watching Johnny eat cheesecake was like viewing a dangerous high-wire circus act where the guys wore form-fitting, spangled leotards; she couldn't look away.

"What?" Johnny caught her staring. "Did I get some on my chin?" He frantically dabbed himself with his napkin.

Sara almost wished that he had left a smidgeon on the corner of his mouth for his tongue to seek out and enjoy, or perhaps for her to wipe away.

"No, no. I just—I just couldn't help noticing how much you're into the cheesecake, that's all." She pointed down at her own plate. "The key lime is out of this world." She took a small bite, sipped ice water to temper the tart flavor, then asked suspiciously, "You don't think I'm a stalker, do you?"

Johnny put his fork down on the table and gazed into Sara's eyes for several seconds without blinking. In surprised reaction, Sara pulled back slightly in her chair. She didn't know what to make of Johnny's focused attention.

Oh, God, he does *think I'm a stalker!*

"Of course you're not a stalker. I have no doubt that you'll write a great letter to him," he said. "Sara, you've come up with some crazy ideas in your time. But when you set your mind to doing something, no matter how crazy, it gets done." Johnny slapped his large hand on the table for emphasis. "You're a woman with a mission."

"You're making fun of me."

"*Au contraire*, lovely lady, I'm merely stating the truth." He spoke in a faux British accent that only made Sara more suspicious of his motives. When Johnny saw Sara's stone-faced reaction, he quickly changed his approach. "Come on, Sara. Remember last Easter when you decided that you needed to catch those teenagers who were stealing decorations from your front lawn?"

"They kept taking my giant plastic eggs! I love those mutant eggs. They look like they might hatch dinosaurs."

"So you went out and bought more eggs, then stayed up almost until dawn, waiting behind the shrubs. All so you could scare the pants off a bunch of poor high-school kids already strung out on Skittles and Red Bull."

"Poor? They were laughing and singing to wake the dead!"

"They were until you jumped out and shrieked like a banshee."

Sara laughed. "They thought the headless horseman was after them." She smiled at the memory. "Those hoodlums didn't dare to come back."

"That's exactly what I was trying to say. When you feel that justice needs to be done, nothing gets in your way." Johnny said it as if he was actually proud of her.

Sara blushed, secretly flattered by the compliment. It was a classic Johnny maneuver, making her feel good about things, even when she had entered the "Oh, God, what have I done?" stage.

Having Johnny Nash back in her life after all their years apart was bittersweet. They had been high-school sweethearts for a year. Johnny was her first love, the first guy to show her the wonder of a kiss and the warmth of a tender embrace. But he was a senior with male hormones popping all over the place like firecrackers, and she was a naïve sophomore who was desperately trying to hold firm to her good-girl status. There would be no stealing to second base with Sara, and so Johnny had his heart (or at least his body) stolen by a senior girl who was willing to round the bases as often as he liked. Sara was devastated when he broke up with her and took the other girl to the senior prom. That summer Sara climbed a tree in her backyard and filled notebooks with gloomy poetry.

Johnny went to college upstate to study business administration, and Sara rarely saw him again, except for a few times the next summer when he careened around town in his convertible with his buddies. Sara eventually heard through her mother's grapevine that Johnny had married Denise, his prom date, and that they had settled down in their old hometown.

Sara, for some reason, never stayed in one place or with one person for very long after college in Connecticut. She roamed from town to town, job to job, one failed relationship after another, until she married Nick. It had seemed the right thing to do at the time. She and Nick had already shared an apartment in New York City, splitting expenses and watching the same television shows. It just seemed logical to take the relationship to the next stage. Unfortunately, Nick had hidden a key component of his personality until after the wedding. He became a domineering bastard, monitoring everything Sara said and did once the vows were exchanged. It seemed impossible that the man who had once lavished her with gifts and attention could turn into this narcissist,

and she tried everything in order to please him including trying
to change herself. But, of course, nothing worked, and she fled the
marriage, emotionally drained and abused. She had always thought
she was too smart to end up with a man who would hurt her, but
she learned that abuse comes in many disguises, and anyone can fall
victim.

In the aftermath of her divorce, a homing instinct led Sara back
to Pittsburgh, hoping to find old friends and lick her wounds. Her
mother and sister were there, and now Gertie, Nicole, and Sara were
closer than ever. Work introduced her to Jen and Char, Joe Norris
had drifted in from...*somewhere*...awash in Axe body spray and
clothes from the pages of *GQ*. Pittsburgh was an unlikely breeding
ground for metrosexuals, but there Joe was.

And then there was Johnny. Again.

It hadn't taken long for him to hear that Sara was back in
town, nor for him to plant his workboots on her doorstep. His own
marriage to Denise was long-ago dissolved, so Sara and Johnny, both
single and childless, were free to renew their friendship. However,
Sara wasn't about to let herself get entangled with Johnny on a
romantic level. She had learned her lesson back in high school.
There was no way she was going to allow him, or any other man,
to break her heart again. Besides, she'd heard rumors about one
or two of Johnny's dalliances in Brighton Park and surrounding
neighborhoods. He wasn't going to make a poetry-writing fool out of
her a second time.

"Do you know why I'm writing Adam West this letter?" Sara asked.

"I confess I don't have a clue. But I do know it means something
to you, and that's enough for me." He scraped his fork across the
plate to gather the remaining cheesecake bits. " Why is my opinion
on this so important to you anyway?"

Sara's nerves went taught at his hopeful gaze. She raced to
get her words out. "It's not that I need your approval or anything
like that. I just wanted...some feedback. I'm bouncing my thoughts
against people to see what sticks."

"And how many people are wandering around town with Sara's
thoughts stuck to their flesh like so many alien spider-webs?"

"A couple," she said self-consciously.

"Okay, so what are you going to say in this soul-baring bearing letter to Adam? Here, I'll start it…Dear Mr. West…"

"Very original."

"Well what *are* you going to say?"

"Whatever it is, I'm not letting you write it for me. You're putting me on the spot, Johnny. I need to think about this—get the right words and sentiments."

"But it's a fan letter, right?" Johnny said. "You'll tell him how you've enjoyed his movies and that old *Batman* television show. That you wish him success in his future projects." He spread his arms dramatically. "Then you'll wind up by confessing that you want to marry him and have his babies."

Sara shrieked, right in the middle of the Cheesecake Factory. "I knew it! You faker!"

Johnny's laughter carried across to the tables next to them. People turned to stare at them, and Sara tried to quiet him. Johnny just kept laughing in a deep baritone. Even his green eyes were dancing with merriment.

"I hate you, Johnny. I really do," Sara whispered vehemently. She wanted to get good and mad at him, but his convulsive laughter was infectious. She began to giggle in spite of herself, then cleared her throat several times to gain some semblance of dignity.

"I thought you were being supportive, but now I see it's all a joke." Challenging Johnny's chivalrous streak was usually a successful tactic. Guilt did its work. Johnny's laughter stopped, but his smile remained.

"Oh, Sara, come on. I *was* trying to support you, but my imagination got the better of me. I'm sorry, really I am." He held his hands out in mute supplication. Sara chose to ignore the remnant of a chuckle that he had to choke down.

"Okay, I guess you're forgiven." They sat in amiable silence as they finished their cheesecake.

"Don't you think that it's a little unusual for a woman your age to write a fan letter?" Johnny asked from out of the blue. Sara's forgiveness of the moment before waned, and she considered whacking him over the head with her purse.

"I'm not any particular *age*. And no, I don't. And it's not a fan letter. It's a letter to thank him for his contributions to my childhood, for his being a part of my adolescence, you know—my formative years."

"Does anybody else from your past rate a letter?"

Sara wondered if Johnny was fishing for validation of his own importance to her past. She wasn't willing to grant it.

"Nope. Just Adam West." She put her fork down. The cheesecake finished, she was beginning to feel the bulge in the waistline of her stretch jeans. This, combined with Johnny's questions, made her uncomfortable.

"So Adam West is the symbol for all that was right about your childhood," Johnny continued.

"Yes, I guess so. And for all that I've become as a result."

"Uh-huh. I see. Well then, why couldn't he have influenced you to become Catwoman? I would have written Adam West a fan letter for that." He wiggled his eyebrows cartoonishly. Sara found it funny that spandex was the fabric of choice for most men, as long as they didn't have to shoehorn their own bodies into it. And she wondered if his interest was in her, or only in her in a cat-suit. Either way, he must be delusional if he believed she could carry off the sleek and sexy Julie Newmar look.

She did not want to deal in delusions. "How's the carpentry business?" she asked.

Johnny took the hint. "I'm working on a project for a new restaurant over at the Waterfront. They commissioned tables and chairs, seating for around fifty. It'll be a nice intimate place, sort of like a bistro for the daytime lunch crowd."

It had surprised everyone in town when Johnny had left the field of business after his divorce and had begun a small carpentry business. It had surprised them again when his business turned out to be lucrative. He had a talent for working the wood in his capable hands.

"That should keep you busy for a while," Sara said.

"You're not kidding. I'm having to contract out to meet the demand. I won't be having too many days off in the next few months." He closely watched Sara's reaction to this statement. She coached her face into a neutral, friendly expression. She enjoyed hanging out with Johnny and was sorry that their fun would be limited, especially now that the weather was getting warmer. But she didn't want him to think she would be sitting by the phone waiting for him to be available.

"You'll have to give me a call when you come up for air," she said lightly. "Maybe we'll do Kennywood." Kennywood was a Pittsburgh tradition: an old-time amusement park complete with rickety, wooden coasters, an Old Mill boat ride to hide stolen smooches, and a penny arcade where games now cost 50 cents.

Johnny pursed his lips into the semblance of a smile and said, "Kennywood. Yeah. Maybe we'll do that." He looked for their waitress, digging for his wallet.

Sara blurted, "What do you hear from the ex?"

Ouch. Kennywood had been a conversation-stopper. Too many memories. Sara was attempting to jump-start things by inviting a dirty tell-all. She kicked herself for lack of subtlety. And for letting Johnny think she gave a damn what his ex was up to.

"Nothing much at all, thank goodness."

"I thought Denise was trying to get you to build her a new deck." Sara knew "the ex" was always trying to get something free out of Johnny, in the hopes of rekindling their relationship. Johnny had long ago discovered that Denise was still seeing the guy that Johnny had caught her with, sans clothing, in the wedding bed that he had carved with his own hands.

"*Trying.* Tried. Failed. Why would I help her with anything when she's engaged to that butthead, Larry," said Johnny.

"They're engaged? Are you okay with that?"

"Sara, I'm ecstatic. I hope that they live happily ever after... and leave me the hell alone." He gave Sara a slow smile. "That numbskull better be handy with a hammer. Denise is quite the little home-wrecker."

Sara snorted at his lame joke, but was relieved that Johnny wasn't upset by Denise's engagement. Now he could move on, forgetting his failed marriage, and owing Denise no favors. Sara knew that she was lucky in that respect; *her* ex lived hundreds of miles away and, truth be told, didn't care what she was up to. Once she'd faced the pain of that immutable fact, it she realized it was a blessing.

"It's funny, both of us sitting here decades after high school, successful in our careers."

"And losers in our marriages," he added.

She reached across the table and put her hand on his sleeve. "I'm glad you're still here, Johnny. Friends forever."

"I know." He laid his hand over Sara's and squeezed it gently. "Now let's pay the check so you can go home and write that letter to Mr. West."

"And feed the dog," she agreed.

CHAPTER FOUR

"Listen, Dog, I'm trying to get some work done around here. You're not helping by getting me all tangled up in this leash."

But the dog was determined to help. By tangling Sara in his leash. So, with a "No! Stop, go back!" Sara toppled to the kitchen floor and landed, sitting, between her garbage can and a dog who appeared to be both spring-loaded and laced with amphetamines.

Sara refused to call the dog by his given name, Arf. She didn't want to get too familiar with him. With any luck, Char would find him a new home, and Sara would be done with him and all his...dog stuff, which included the leash that had just wrapped twice around her legs and lassoed her to the ground.

Mouthing words she hoped her kindergartners did not know, Sara unwound the leash and groaned as she stood up. She opened the kitchen door. "Out you go, you little troublemaker." The dog shot out ahead of her. "Dog has left the building," she muttered as she walked across the small fenced-in yard to the stake she had recently pounded into the ground. She wanted to be doubly sure that she kept the dog safe; so although she had fencing, she used the secured leash as well. Despite the dog's efforts at alternately pulling away from her and licking her ears, she looped the leash through the stake and tied a secure knot. "There you go, Dog. Knock yourself out. And, by the way, you're a sloppy kisser." She walked resolutely back to the house, and closed the door without a backward glance.

Dear Mr. West,

Hello, Sir! I've wanted to write this letter every day since I saw your latest Batman movie. I hope you'll stick with me as I share my feelings. You see, my admiration for you has inspired my life, and it's been a wild ride.

Several weeks ago, in a conversation with a friend, I learned that you had done a movie called Return to the Batcave. *My friend loaned me the DVD, and I sat back for an evening of fun and mayhem.*

I didn't realize what an incredible impact this movie would have on me. I just had to tell you about all this for two reasons. One, I couldn't let another day go by without thanking you for such a delightful performance—both in this movie and in your classic, 1960s TV series. And two, there's some unfinished business that demands my attention.

As I watched Return to the Batcave, *I, well I guess I kind of lost myself in it. I got to thinking. How long ago was it that I watched the* Batman *TV show? How could you be doing a retrospective film about a decades-old show, when it was only yesterday that I watched you saving Gotham City in* Batman *reruns?*

I realized that, in my mind, I had locked you in the form you'd taken in 1966—a dashing, leotard-clad Adonis.

Whatever happened to the decades between now and then? I've had to face that I've also traveled forward in time. You've gotten older. I've gotten older. We've both gotten older. This passage of years seemed like the blink of an eye, and that unsettles me.

So I took to Google to learn what you have been doing during the decades that I was lost in a world that seems so far from planet Earth.

I spent hours reading about your acting career. I was surprised— even angry—that, after Batman *ended in '68, instead of being scooped up for other roles, the studios decided that you were too closely identified with your superhero role. It didn't seem to matter that you had been nominated for Best New Male Actor of the Year in 1967. When* Batman *ended, the studio handed over your cape and utility belt and firmly closed the gate behind you.*

You've said that you were "married to the cowl," and it certainly seems that way since you did countless appearances in the Batman *costume to make ends meet. I remember when I was in high school*

I heard that you were doing car shows and mall openings wearing your Batman costume, and I wondered why you were still clinging to your cape and tights. Now I know you had to do these gigs in order to survive. With these superhero appearances, you were able to remain a role model for children, and this probably helped you through the lean years. I admire that you never gave up trying to develop your career, and now your drive is paying off.

Through my research, I learned of your professional accomplishments, photos of you through the years at various functions, bunches of fan clubs and websites dedicated to the Batman *phenomenon.*

I also learned that Adam West was quite the ladies' man. He cut a wide swath through the female contingent in Hollywood during the Batman *years. I imagine the adoration of millions of fans both here in America and abroad was a stimulating experience.*

So now the question is, what does Batman *have to do with me, an average American gal?*

I'm amazed that I've lost track of something that truly meant something to me when I was young. I'm sure I wasn't aware of the influence that your TV show and your acting had on me at the time. As people do with their heroes, I took you for granted and assumed that you would be there, and be the same, forever.

That was wrong.

I don't want to go another day without crediting you and your Batman character for your positive impact on my life. When my first love, Johnny, walked through the door of my parents' home in Pittsburgh, Pennsylvania, family lore has it that my mother greeted him, then dragged my father into the kitchen to tell him, "Oh my god, she's brought home Batman."

I honestly hadn't been conscious of the fact that Johnny was a dead ringer for you, Mr. West. Now when I look back at the pictures of Johnny and me as teenagers, it's as obvious as the nose on my face. Although the relationship lasted only a few months, he's still a friend in my life, and people still ask him, "Are you...?"

I've come to see that I also have an ingrained sense of right and wrong, a set of values that guides me like a constant compass in my job as a kindergarten teacher.

I think that when I was younger I needed to believe that there could be a world where right always triumphed and the bad guys were hauled off to jail after every crime. I still wish for that Gotham City and Batman in this often-crazy world, but my grown-up common sense understands that reality is much more complex and that sometimes the bad guys do get away.

Batman *nurtured my love of adventure. Although instead of fighting off the weekly villains and their fantastical evil plots, I have come face to face with a charging moray in the Caribbean and survived a screaming descent by parachute from a perfectly good airplane.*

Now I would like to address the Adam West that you are today, the actor that I have rediscovered.

I'm so pleased that you've been sought after by the movie studios and have become an icon to a new generation. I've seen you on TV sitcoms—appearing as yourself. Your performances are so plentiful that I can find you on some channel on any day of the week.

People like me want to pay homage to you. You are a true icon, and you deserve this recognition.

So, how is it, Mr. West, that you look decades younger than your actual age? You make 80 look like the new 50.

Okay, so maybe this is turning into a fan girl letter! While my intention has been to acknowledge you, it has also helped me face the passage of time. I want you to know that your influence in my life is one of your legacies.

(Of course, you now have your own star on the walk of fame in Hollywood, and that is a most fitting tribute.)

Thank you for it all, Mr. West.

Sincerely, Sara Goode

Sara removed the pages of the letter from the printer tray, signed the last page, and stuffed them into an envelope. She slapped on a handful of stamps, probably double the necessary postage. She didn't want to take any chances that this letter wouldn't make it to its destination.

She peeked out of the window on her kitchen door and saw that Dog was contentedly lying on the ground in the sunshine, snuffling at the grass and bugs. Satisfied that he was safe, she hopped into her Mini Cooper and drove the three miles to the Brighton Park Post Office in the center of town. Tossing the letter down the mailbox chute made her feel good. She had done what she had set out to accomplish; she had thanked Mr. West. A side benefit was that she had gained some insight into herself.

Now Sara could relax and maybe spend the rest of the day at home watching *Batman* episodes on her Blu-ray player and keeping Dog off the couch. She felt like such a geek. If she wasn't careful, she'd soon be reading vintage comic books and collecting action figures.

After a few hours of binge-watching *Batman,* she promised herself that she would work on creating some motivating lesson plans for her kindergarten students. She needed to leave Gotham City at some point and come back down to Earth as mild-mannered Sara Goode.

Oh, and of course she'd have to find time to take Dog for a walk. The sooner that mutt got a new home, the happier Sara would be. Of that, she was certain.

CHAPTER FIVE

Sara had a suspicion that the general population had no idea that kindergarten was no longer fun. When she was a child, kindergarten was the set of training wheels that helped kids learn to balance their future school life. Kids learned to play beside each other at the sand table without flinging cups of the grit into each other's eyes. They learned to line up like little soldiers and walk quietly down the halls. They even learned to sit in hard wood chairs at a table—but only for short periods of time. Recess was the shining apex of the day, with kids running in packs back and forth across the playground, climbing the monkey bars and playing Red Rover.

In those days, when you graduated from kindergarten, you were a civilized being with a firm knowledge of the ABCs and a handle on the difference between right and wrong. The choice of whether to use the left or right hand over the heart during the morning pledge may still have been a bit of a puzzle, but they generally passed you on to first grade anyway.

Kindergarten is not like that anymore. The children sit on those wood chairs all day, every day. They learn to read, write and do arithmetic. If a child doesn't come to the first day of kindergarten with a firm knowledge of how to read and write the alphabet, he might as well not show up at all. Children are expected to learn to read books, struggle through math with addition and subtraction and write stories with their own inventive spelling.

The inventive spelling made Sara the craziest of all. She figured if she was going to teach the kids, she might as well do it the right way. But heaven forbid if she stifled a child's creativity by asking him to follow the rules of grammar and spelling.

Then there was the "Morals and Values" curriculum, which never failed to make her seethe. Teaching the proscribed behavioral lessons felt like pounding standards of Political Correctness into her little students' brains. It was like something Stalin would have ordered.

Sara hadn't signed on for this "advanced kindergarten" when she had gone to college and earned her teaching degree. Back then, things were pretty sane, educationally speaking. Sara arrived in her first classroom, a bright-eyed, freshly minted kindergarten teacher, ready to gently welcome the youth of America. But, over the years, the creep of insidious standardized testing had changed the focus from the children to the bottom line.

Sara hated the changes. How was a child to be expected to sit for six straight hours a day? It was no wonder the teachers needed all these new behavior curricula. The kids were going batty because they weren't allowed to move. A teachers's opinion counted for nothing, but she had come up with ways to make her classroom more child-friendly.

For example, spring was the time of year when Sara was supposed to be introducing phonics to her class. She could do it the usual and expected way by writing word-families *ad nauseum* on the chalk board—"sit, fit, hit, how, now, cow." But, it was *spring*, and there was no way she was going to spend another minute within the confining brick walls of May View Elementary School.

She whipped up some word-beginnings and word-endings on note cards, punched holes in the cards and strung yarn through the holes. She marched her class outside to the school horticultural area—the former playground—a sophisticated name for a few scraggly sunflowers and a lot of gangly plants that looked like weeds but were labeled "nature preserve." Each student, a card around his or her little neck, ran happily through the graveled paths, seeking out a friend whose own card would match to make a complete word.

Sara thought that her lesson was absolutely brilliant. The students were having fun while learning, and they were getting their lungs filled with fresh spring air.

Suddenly, Sara heard a cry from classroom prima donna Rebecca Swenson.

"Mrs. Goode!" Rebecca's voice shrilled across the yard, threatening to make the preserved weeds wilt. Sara detested being called "Missus." She was fine being a Miss, but Principal Johnson insisted that all teachers be called "Missus" despite their marital status. Asking "Even the men?" had not won Sara any points.

"Mrs. Goode!" Rebecca shrieked again, though Sara was now right beside her.

"What's the problem?" Sara tried to sound sympathetic, but she never could quite muster the requisite warmth with Rebecca.

"Jeffrey said a bad word," Rebecca announced with a prim little smile.

Sara spun around to find the offending boy. "Jeffrey, did you, or did you not, say a bad word?" Tattlers often reported imagined crimes, and Sara would consider Jeffrey innocent unless he admitted his guilt. She had a special gift for shaking down the truth from her students, and they all knew it. She could look them straight in the eye, with a slight head tilt to the left, and stare deep into their little souls.

Jeffrey eyes went wide and threatened to leak tears. "No, Mrs. Goode! I didn't say nothin'."

Sara's gut saying that Jeffrey was being honest, she turned back to Rebecca. "Clearly there has been some misunderstanding."

Rebecca had reported the transgression with hands on hips, an expression of disgust on her face. On any other child, such an expression would look out of place. Rebecca's face seemed to be designed by nature to envisage disgust. She raised one hand and pointed it at Jeffrey.

"He went up to Charlie and made a bad word with his letter card."

Sara read Jeffrey's beginning word card with the letters "sh." She then spotted Charlie's word ending card printed with the letters "it."

Sara's gaze swept the three children before her. "It was an accident. It was nobody's fault, and if I hear anyone talking about this or repeating the word in school, that person will be in big trouble."

Rebecca was gloating at her success tattling on the boys. Sara's blood pressure ratcheted up. "And that includes you, too, Rebecca." Rebecca, stunned by this dire threat, took a miscalculated step forward and landed on her bottom. Sara had no time for coddling and sympathy. This was an emergency situation.

"Children! Letter cards off and placed in a pile at my feet. Right now!" Sara called across the field. The rest of the children ran over and deposited their cards in front of her. She quickly scanned the school windows. Heaven help her if some eagle-eyed co-worker—or, worse, *student*—had caught the historic creation of "the bad word." She didn't see any onlookers, but it was hard to tell with the sun glancing off the glass panels that were angled outwards to let in the spring air.

"Um, you all did a great job. Now let's head back to the classroom, and we'll write down the words you made." She could only pray that no other "bad" words had been created without her knowledge. "Jeffrey, help Rebecca up. Charlie, you bring in the cards." Sara turned and marched back to the door, hoping that her ducklings had fallen into a line behind her. Her head was pounding and she could think of only one word to express her anxiety that *someone* with authority would hear of this incident.

That word had been formed by Jeffrey and Charlie with their cards.

Back in the classroom, her headache fading in the shadow of a few extra-strength aspirin, Sara watched her students industriously transcribing their word lists. She slowly strolled the classroom, patting the shoulder of an occasional child, like Bobby Moore and Suzie Elmore, who was especially focused on the task.

In the corner of the room furthest from her, she observed two boys whispering heatedly. "Boys," Sara called. "Please be quiet or you'll have to stay in for recess." This was the nuclear threat, and it usually worked well, thank goodness. Following through on it meant giving up her prep period, and she didn't like to do that. When else was she to get her on-line shopping done? Unfortunately, this looked like one of those occasions when she'd have to carry out her threat. The boys started frantically grabbing at each other's hands across their table, resulting in flying papers and pencils. Sara was beside them in a flash.

"What part of 'be quiet' do you not understand?" Sara laid a hand on the shoulder of each boy, invoking the power given to teachers down through the ages. It included a gentle touch paired with a fearsome snarl. "Hmm?"

Larry, a dark-curly-haired moppet, whined, "It's mine. He took it from me."

Joshua, sporting a Mohawk and camouflage, countered Larry's claim with a sneer. "No, I didn't. It's my car, and I want it back."

Sara would have to play Judge Judy to sort out this mess, and what with lunch only minutes away, she wasn't in the mood for a session of "he said/he said." There was only one course of action.

"Give me the car. Whoever has it, give it to me now."

Joshua reluctantly extended his arm with a fist tightly wrapped around the car towards Sara. "I'm going to tell my dad."

"That better not be a threat, mister, 'cause there's a week's worth of after-school detentions waiting for you if it is."

Joshua looked as if he might hold his ground, toughie that he was, but then decided to let his "better" nature take over. "Here," he muttered and pushed the car into her hand. "It's a piece of crap anyway." Sara chose to ignore the crude language and slipped the car into her pants pocket.

"You boys know that toys from home aren't allowed in the classroom. I'm going to have to put this in my drawer until the end of the school year." The drawer of confiscated contraband had become quite full as of the school year approached. Sara had to admit that she enjoyed playing with the hand-held electronic games after school sometimes. "Now finish your word lists."

As she walked back to her desk, the lunch bell rang. Sara's students jumped up, their chairs scraping against the linoleum floor.

"Write your name on your papers and put them on my desk as you leave."

In a whirlwind of denim, sneakers, sparkly headbands and flailing limbs, the children took leave of her classroom. Sara sat down to flip through their papers, hoping upon blind hope that all the words would be legitimate. It took only a few minutes to alleviate her fears. Every scribbled and scratched word could be spoken aloud in a house of worship. She sighed audibly in relief. It was then that she remembered the car she'd taken from Joshua. Sara reached into her pocket and took out…a Batmobile. For a long moment she marveled at the coincidence then she tossed the car into her desk drawer. It was lunchtime for her, too.

The populace of the teachers' lunchroom was divided into groups just like the cliques in the school lunchroom. There were the new, pretty teachers, otherwise known as the "Young Darlings," who sat near the windows, basking in the sunshine and planning weddings or island vacations. In the back of the lunchroom, near the snack machines, sat the "Teacher Nerds," the dedicated, over-enthusiastic teachers who constantly debated nature vs.nurture theories of intelligence and were the first to volunteer for after-school science and classic books clubs. The old-timers, dubbed "The Queenies," claimed the center tables, eating microwaved leftovers from the previous night's family dinner.

Jen, Char and Sara belonged to the "Norms." Anyway, that's what they called themselves after giving names to the other groups. They were the ones who didn't fit into any other category and preferred it that way. Char could have taken a place by the window as a "Young Darling," but she seemed content with her less-fabulous friends. They shared an old, overstuffed couch with a wobbly coffee table in front of it. The table was scattered with outdated catalogs and magazines. The couch gave them a good overall view of the lunchroom. As the saying goes, it's best to keep your back to the walls when you're around the enemy. Every teacher alive knew that the lunchroom was a hive of deceit and villainy; no one's reputation or credentials were safe within its gossip-filled walls.

Sara landed between Jen and Char on the couch. "What's the buzz?"

"I was just telling Jen about my Picasso lesson." Charlotte said.

Sara shook her head. *Honestly, Picasso for Kindergartners. There should be some kind of law.* "Whatever happened to finger painting and paper mosaics? You know, this morning I was flashing back to when I first started teaching and the kids had things like free recess and field trips to the pickle factory."

Charlotte laughed. "Did they have pickles in the age of dinosaurs?"

Sara had to smile. "No, right after that."

"Fortunately, there's that creative element in the Picasso projects—they can place the eyes and noses wherever they want." Charlotte sighed. "They won't be marked down for forgetting to draw arms and legs."

"Speaking of creativity," Sara said quietly, "I had an innovative lesson that bombed today."

Charlotte perked up. "Oh, what happened?"

Jen tossed her egg salad sandwich on the table and raised her hand in the air. "Ooh, ooh, let me!" She swallowed her last bite and wiped her mouth with a paper napkin. "Okay, Char. What's a word that rhymes with 'fit' but begins with 'sh?'"

Sara stared at Jen in horror. "Noooooo! You didn't. You saw?"

Jen nodded.

"Where were you?" Sara's heart was threatening to beat right out of her chest.

"In the office. Principal Johnson's meeting room, to be exact. I was looking out the window when I was supposed to be listening to him. I was wishing I could be with your students—enjoying the sunshine, running around …making *bad* words." She emphasized "bad" like a self-righteous old church lady.

"Did Principal Johnson see them?" Sara begged to know.

"Nope. His back was to the windows. Besides, he had bigger problems to deal with." Jen picked up her sandwich again and took a big bite.

Sara turned to Charlotte and tried to give her an explanation of the morning's debacle. "Each student had to match cards with another student to make a word."

"And the little angels came up with interesting combinations?" Charlotte asked.

"Oh, yeah, way too interesting. I am so screwed. If anybody else saw what happened, I'll probably get put on probation." Sara scanned the lunchroom to see if anyone was looking at her suspiciously. Was Cissie Bolton avoiding her gaze? Two other teachers from Cissie's "Queenie" table definitely stole glances before darting their eyes away. *Great,* thought Sara. Cissie had a motor mouth to put Oprah's to shame, *and* her third-grade classroom overlooked the courtyard.

Oh, yes, Sara was indeed up a creek without a paddle.

She whispered to Jen. "Are you sure the Principal didn't see?" If confronted, she would deny everything. It would be her word against Cissie Bolton's, and everyone knew Cissie was a liar. No way did she make those "famous" chocolate chip cookies from scratch.

"Listen, I told you. Principal Johnson was too upset about something else." Jen gestured for the girls to bring their heads in closer. "Someone is hacking into the online grade books and changing grades."

Charlotte and Sara looked at each other in surprise. This was something that might happen in a high school, but at May View Elementary School? It was impossible to imagine.

"Some student is changing grades to A's and B's?" Sara ventured.

Jen shook her head. "No, it's the opposite. Someone is targeting the smart kids and making their grades lower."

"I bet somebody's older brother or sister is in on this. It's too complicated for our students." Sara certainly couldn't see any of her little ragamuffins involved in a caper like this.

Char moaned. "Does this mean we all have to go through our grade books and resubmit our grades?"

"I think Principal Johnson will be calling an after-school meeting for the teachers about this," said Jen.

Sara saw a silver lining in this scenario. "If it keeps Johnson busy and off my back, I'll gladly redo my grades—and yours, Char."

"I'm going to hold you to that."

"This is a job for a Caped Crusader," Jen said quietly.

Sara was about to twist the cap off her diet peach iced tea when she realized what Jen had just said.

"*Wha-a-t?*"

Jen smiled mischievously. "I said—this is a job for a Caped Crusader."

"Why in the world would you say that?" Then a thought dawned on Sara. "Have you been talking to Joe?"

"Funny thing," said Jen. "I was at the Depot yesterday picking up a few items for the office, when who do I bump into but Joe Norris. He was putting in an order for computer paper. Isn't that a coincidence? We're both in charge of offices, and we both needed office supplies."

"Uncanny," agreed Sara. "Regular *Unsolved Mysteries* stuff."

"*Unsolved Mysteries?*" asked Char. "Is that a show or something?"

Sara ignored her. She was too annoyed with Jen. "I guess you two had a wonderful time talking about me and my Batman thing."

Jen shrugged. "It did happen to come up in the conversation."

"I really am always the last to know anything about everything," said Char. "Is this about the movie I lent you?" she asked.

"Sort of," said Sara.

"But Joe and I talked about other things, too," Jen continued, "He's really knowledgeable about computers."

"He's an I.T. specialist," said Sara. "It's kind of a thing."

"Maybe I'll ask his advice about tracking down the hackers."

"You could be Nancy Drew to his Hardy boy," Sara said.

Jen blushed a little just then. Sara decided to keep a close eye on those two to see if romance was budding. She turned to Char and asked, "So? Don't you want to know about your dog? I've had him for *quite a few days* now."

Char lit up. "Oh! Right! How is Arf?"

Sara suppressed a growl. *Not a trace of guilt.*

"He now goes by the name Dog. He's... alive. We have achieved a détente. He doesn't chew up my couch pillows, and I don't forget to let him back in the house after he does his business. I'm guessing that you haven't made any progress in finding him a new owner, have you?" Sara glared at Char, hoping to burn into her some motivation to get the dog out of her house.

Char smiled tentatively. "I—I can't thank you enough for boarding Arf. My relationship with Mitchell is a dream, now that he isn't sneezing and itching at hives all over his body."

"Mmm-hmm," Sara said.

" I...haven't exactly had time to start looking for a new home for Arf." To Sara's angrily flashing eyes, she said, hopefully, "I promise I'll start tomorrow?"

Sara was cold. "What's wrong with today? Dog has to go. Nothing against him personally, but I prefer to remain unattached to all needy creatures—including men and animals."

"Fine, I'll put an ad in a few newspapers this afternoon. I sure wish I could have kept him. Arf is so sweet."

"Give me a chocolate bar instead. It's satisfying, and it doesn't leave hair balls on the kitchen floor."

"Eww," Char said.

Sara gathered her trash and stood. "It's not all puppy kisses and walks in the park, you know." Over her shoulder, she added, "Sometimes it's hair balls and dog farts."

CHAPTER SIX

One Friday afternoon a month, the Goode women bonded at their favorite beauty shop in the south hills of Pittsburgh. Sara, her mother, Gertie, and her sister, Nicole, swapped stories and indulged in their God-given right to interfere with the natural growth (and color) of their hair. The shop was run by the Mataluski sisters, two friendly, chatty gals who were Sara's age and who really knew their way around a dye job. Their dear-departed, Polish mother had given them glorious, feminine names, Danielle and Joelle. But fate, or the down-home Pittsburgh ways of the girls, led them to be called Danny and Jojo. The sisters ran a cute shop—Cool Cuts—nestled among other mom-and-pop stores along Potomac Road in Dormont. The store's name always reminded Sara of cold cut sandwiches with the local Isaly's chipped ham piled high on a Kaiser roll. Danny and Jojo had married their blue-collar sweethearts right out of high school, with their full lives supplied evidenced by family photographs engulfing the walls of the shop.

On Saturday mornings, Cool Cuts hosted what was known in the neighborhood as "the blue-hair stampede." Senior ladies from all over town descended, and all four of the shop's stations were in full swing. Pittsburgh, besides being a center of commerce, a backdrop for the arts and a sports haven for Steelers, Penguins and Pirates fans, is home to more senior citizens than any other locale in the United States, except for Dade County in southern Florida.

Fortunately for the Goode women, early Friday evening was a slow night at Cool Cuts, and they were always the only customers in the salon.

Gertie was getting a perm from Danny. She would soon be stinking up the place with the noxious setting solution. Nicole was waiting for her manicure and pedicure from Jojo, who was first mixing a batch of dye in a "totally perfect color" for Sara. Both Mataluski sisters were in the back, which left the Goodes a few moments' privacy. Sara took the opportunity to whisper the problems at school.

Principal Johnson had sworn all of the teachers and school staff to secrecy regarding the hacking. It was a matter that required skilled detective work—both on and off the computer—without the general public's knowledge. Principal Johnson would, in due time, inform the community of parents and students. But the investigators needed lead time to investigate, and perhaps, surprise the culprits.

Sara knew her family was too far out of the loop to be a threat to the investigation, so she'd spoken freely.

"I bet Jen is excited," observed Sara's sister. Nicky knew Jen from occasional party nights at the clubs. "She just loves a good mystery, doesn't she?"

"Oh, yeah, Jen's beside herself. It's all she can talk about," Sara smiled to herself. "And you know what? The police are really using her expertise—"

"Is changing a few grades a police matter?" asked Gertie.

"We're not actually sure, but Principal Johnson thinks it is. Maybe the police just got tired of the phone calls and sent an officer. Anyway, Jen's the only one who really knows the school database. It seems that her days of being a self-appointed school super-sleuth are paying off."

"What does the principal think about Jen spending time with the police? I mean, is she getting her *job* done, or just trying to get a date with a young cop?" Gertie asked.

"He's fine with it. As far as he's concerned, controlling the potential scandal *is* Job One. He wants things wrapped up before the end of the school year. He's hoping any possible backlash from parents about network security should be minimal because of summer vacation." Sara shook her head. "Personally, I think he's deluding himself."

Nicky, not looking up from the manicurist's display card of new shades of red nail polish, said, "Oh, these things have a way of blowing over."

"Jen's even got my friend, Joe, involved. He's a computer geek."

"Among other things," Nicole said. Before Sara could stand up for Joe, Nicky was waving a bright, redder than red, nail polish bottle in front of her. "Hey, how about Candy Apple?" she asked.

"That's a bit too... *red* for my tastes," Sara said. "I like the mauves. They're pretty without screaming 'harlot.'"

Nicky frowned at her in annoyance.

"What are you trying to say, Sara?"

"Just that I'm a school teacher, not a runway model."

"Even schoolteachers have the right to make a personal statement."

"Uh-huh. And I will continue to make my statements verbally, thank you very much."

"Ha! That's your problem—too much talking and not enough action," said Nicky. "My God, the most interesting thing in your life is a pee-wee grade-fixing operation! At least you have a dog now. It shows you're willing to put yourself out there for another living creature. First a dog, then a man."

Sara was perturbed by Nicky's comments, and ready to go a few rounds with her, but Gertie intervened.

"Girls! It's our Friday time. *No bickering.*" Gertie said this at least weekly. Nicky and Sara liked to snarl and scrape, but it was mostly all in good, sisterly fun. They rarely got into a real fight. Indeed, they grudgingly respected each other.

Of course, if Gertie had really wanted peace in the family, she would not have added, "But Nicky's right, Sara. You could stand to perk yourself up a bit more. A brighter lipstick and some colored nail polish can go a long way to catching a man's eye."

"Wha—? I—"

Gertie held up her finger for silence. "Now, Sara, how long has it been since the divorce? Don't you think it's time that you got out there again and met some fellas?"

Nicky replaced the Candy Apple polish and said, "Or even one special 'fella' in particular? Hmm?"

"If you two interfering hens don't back off right now—"

"'Hens?'" wondered Nicky.

"'Interfering?'" demanded Gertie.

"—I'm going to walk through those doors and go straight home! I could be watching reruns of *America's Funniest Videos* and eating Cherry Garcia—"

"And adding inches to your hips," put in Gertie.

"—*right out of the container*...in blissful peace and quiet," finished Sara.

Jojo bustled in from the back room. "Ok, ok, are yins guys gonna kibbitz all evening or is someone gonna get in that chair?" Nicky and Sara shared a private smile. The sisters were always amazed that the Pittsburgh-ese "yins guys" was still being used.

"That would be my cue." Sara slid into Jojo's chair and glanced at the photos of her hairdresser's German shepherd taped to the mirror at her station. There were twice as many pictures of Duke than there were of her kids and husband, Bill. Jojo was nuts about that old, mangy dog. Sara just couldn't see the point.

"I just want highlights around the front, since summer is here. Or will be soon."

Jojo draped a cloth apron, black with pastel polka dots, around Sara's shoulders.

"Did you warsh your hair this morning?"

"Nope. I kept it dirty especially for you."

Jojo's approving glance met Sara's in the mirror. "Good girl. You know that the color will stick better that way."

"Can I have a little trim in the back, too?" Sara asked.

"Sure, after we get Nicky's nails painted." Jojo tweaked Sara's elbow. "We gotta make her gorgeous for the men." Sara rolled her eyes, but the truth was that Nicky, only a year younger than herself, managed to look like a college kid. She was petite like their mother. Her figure was perfect—not an extra ripple or bulge anywhere. When she bent her pretty index finger, men came running. Nicky had been divorced five years, and Gertie had never nagged her to find another man—not when she saw how the guys flocked around her youngest. That left Sara, the Cinderella of the Goode sisters, as Gertie's *special project.*

Nicky, at the wash station, was now flipping through the latest issue of *Cosmo.* "You, know, I'm starting to think that they don't make men like they used to."

Danny came out of the back, vigorously shaking a plastic bottle. "Yins got that right. My Bobby may be the last of the good ones. Gertie, let's go. Time's a-wasting."

"You said it." Gertie scooted up into the chair. She was only five-foot one, and beauty-shop chairs and bar stools could be a challenge for her. "There's a midnight Bingo down at the fire hall tonight, and I don't want to miss it. The jackpot's two thousand dollars."

Sara could practically see the gleam of dollar signs in Gertie's eyes. Her mother had a better social life than she did; Sara would be in bed by midnight.

"Nicky," Sara said, "I think I'd have to agree with you about men. I really miss the days when they were *really* men. Men used to dress in fine suits, and they'd smell so good in aftershave."

"Ugh," Gertie said. "I always hated Brut."

"Or Old Spice," Danny added.

"And don't forget manners. Guys opened doors for women," Jojo said. She squirted a glop of hair dye into her gloved hands and began working the dye into a section of Sara's hair.

Gertie snorted. "You girls want to live in a fairytale. The only guys who were like that were on the TV or in the movies."

"Dad was clean-shaven and well-groomed," Sara remembered. Her father had never worn a tee shirt as a shirt in his life, and he always looked spiffy enough to turn silver heads at the early bird dinners in the surrounding neighborhoods.

Gertie nodded thoughtfully. "That's true. He was an exception."

Nicky flipped a page over in her magazine. "I want a real man, not some scruffy kid in torn jeans with his hair hanging in his face. I want a guy with chiseled features and a strong jaw. Who do the young girls of today have? Justin Bieber? Come on."

Sara had a sudden thought. "Nicky, you used to have a crush on Dr. Kildare."

Danny nodded, "Oh, yes, Richard Chamberlain. Did you see him in *The Thorn Birds*? He was a priest who was in love with this girl."

Gertie sighed, "He was a cutie-patootie."

Sara started—she couldn't remember her mother using such an expression before. "Mom, if memory serves, you always liked Merv Griffin, the host of an afternoon talk show? And I kind of liked Adam West, remember?"

Gertie's eyes took on a faraway look. "Merv. He had it all—personality, looks, money."

Nicky smacked the Cosmo magazine on her knee. "That's right, Sara! Adam West! I'd forgotten all about him."

Sara sighed deeply. "Yeah, so did I."

Gertie tried to turn towards Sara, but Danny whipped the chair right back so that the perm solution wouldn't run down Gertie's neck. "Jeez Louise, Gert!"

"Sorry." Gertie apologized meekly. "Sara, they could have dropped a bomb outside of our house, and you wouldn't have moved a muscle when you were watching that *Batman* show."

"Funny thing," Sara said nervously, "I, um, actually wrote Mr. West a letter a few days ago."

Nicky laughed. "Why would you do that?"

Sara watched Jojo putting foil around a strip of her gooped hair. "I saw a recent movie he made, *Return to the Batcave*. It just struck me that he was still out there, making movies, and doing guest spots on T.V. shows. I wanted to thank him for giving me such pleasure as Batman."

"Oh, yeah, he gave you pleasure…in your teenage fantasies," Nicky said.

Sara remembered that Joe had made similar comments.

"Nicky, be nice," Gertie said.

"I'm just saying that Sara liked Batman because he was a hottie in that costume," Nicky said.

"Well, I think it's great that you wrote the letter," Gertie said. "I'll bet Adam West was thrilled that someone remembered him after all these years."

"Actually, Mom, from what I could tell from the Internet, he has lots of fans. And he's been doing tons of acting work," Sara said.

"I still think it was a lovely thing to do. Maybe he'll write back. He probably was touched that a younger girl admires him," Gertie said.

Sara let loose with a loud laugh. "First of all, Adam West has no idea how old I am. He's in his eighties, and he's been happily married for about thirty years. For heaven's sake, he has kids that are my age, which by the way, isn't all that young."

"Pfah! That means nothing today. The rules have changed. Age means nothing and marriages come and go like the seasons. I'm sure you'll hear from him."

Her mother's support was a little skewed, but Sara loved her for it. "Well, I wrote the letter, and I now I have to wait and see what happens."

"How did you know where to mail it?" Nicky asked.

"His agent's address was on the Internet; I guess Adam does motivational speeches for charities, and then there are bookings for comic book conventions. He does those, too," Sara said.

"He'll write back. You'll see."

"That would be nice," Sara shrugged without much hope.

"Nicky, maybe you should write to Richard Chamberlain," Sara's mother suggested.

Nicky grimaced. "He's also old, Mom. Also he's gay. And dead."

"Why do you have to be so difficult?" Their mother asked.

The front door swung open, and all turned in unison to see who was arriving during the Friday night graveyard shift.

"Got time to trim a shaggy dog?" Haloed by the glow of street lights beyond the door, in dark blue jeans and a sawdust-covered chamois shirt, was Johnny. His bright cheeks indicated that the evening had turned cool, but his shining eyes showed he was up to mischief. He ran his hands through his thick blonde hair. "So what do you think, girls?"

Jojo put down the highlighting brush and assessed Johnny's hair. "Johnny Nash, I doubt you'd let me touch a hair on your head. We all know that you go down to that barber shop on Main Street."

"Yikes! I've been found out." Johnny's easy smile must have warmed every heart in the room. It warmed Sara's, loath as she was to admit it. "I confess—I saw all the Goode cars in your parking lot and thought I'd stop in to say hello."

Sara hated how glad she was that Johnny had stopped in. Maybe he would stay long enough to make Gertie forget about her daughter's shortcomings in the dating department. But Johnny was off limits, considering their past relationship. Nevertheless, he was easy on the eyes, and he made any girl feel "like a thousand bucks," as Gertie used to say about Sara's dad.

Jojo returned to fussing with Sara's foil-wrapped hair. Sara met Johnny's eyes in the mirror, but he quickly darted his eyes toward Nicky.

"All three Goode girls in one place…I feel like I've won the lottery," he said.

"Or the trifecta," offered Nicky.

"I'm no horse!" Gertie called out.

"Gertie, you're a filly, and you know it!" He leaned in as though to kiss the top of her head, but recoiled. "For the love of all that's honest and true, why does your hair stink like a chemical spill? Are you sure that Danny isn't frying your brains under that stuff?"

Gertie shrugged. "As long as it curls my hair, I don't care if I smell like the inside of your chamois shirt."

"You're a hard woman, Gertie." Johnny turned to the *other* Goode sister. "Hey, Nicky, you're looking prickly—I mean *pretty*—as ever."

Nicky lowered her magazine so that her soft brown eyes fluttered over the top edge of the pages. "Why, Johnny, I think you complimented and insulted me in the same breath."

Johnny laughed. "Prickly is good; it shows spunk. Nobody gets anything over on Nicky Goode."

"You can put money on that, Johnny."

"Rumor has it your flavor of the month is Spanish," Johnny said in a low voice, out of Gertie's hearing.

"Shh." Nicky said. "It's a secret. Carlos thinks he's chasing me, and he will continue to do so until I catch him."

"I'll say no more—scout's honor." Johnny held up two fingers.

Johnny nodded to Danny, who was up to her wrists in Gertie's perm, then approached Sara. She gave him a controlled smile—no sense in giving more than she could expect to get.

"Hello, Sara."

"Hello, Johnny."

Johnny circled her chair, slightly frowning at the layers of foil on her head. "Can you get reception from the mother ship with those things?"

"Funny guy."

"E.T. phone home," Johnny said in a squeaky voice, then he grinned.

"Why don't you go home, and stop bugging us?" Sara demanded.

"Take me to your leader," Johnny continued. He looked proud of himself. Jojo was holding back laughter. If he said one more thing, she was going to let loose with the giggles.

Gertie looked over her glasses and shook her head. "You're like a fox in a henhouse, Johnny. You're rattling all the cages."

"Then my work here is done." Johnny surveyed what was— sadly—now his own domain. "I hate to flirt and run, girls. But I need to get home and shower off this dust and grime."

"Hot date tonight?" Sara asked, curiosity getting the better of her.

Johnny turned and said, "Yeah. With you. At Eat 'n Park. See you there for dinner around eight?"

Sara was stunned by the request. "Well, yeah, I guess. Will I be done here before eight, Jojo?"

"Oh, sure, no problem. In fact, you'll be done by seven-thirty easy." Jojo was hiding a knowing smirk, but Sara saw it as clear as day when she glanced up at her.

It was Sara's turn to sigh. With the vast networking talents of the Mataluski sisters, this tidbit would get around town before sunrise. "Okay, Johnny. Get out of here. I'll see you later."

The door slammed shut as Johnny strode off into the spring evening, leaving Sara planning 50 ways to murder her ex-boyfriend.

CHAPTER SEVEN

Sara muffled a yelp as the toes in her right foot were squashed flat. The Eat 'n Park was practically empty—it was eight in the evening—but it wasn't quiet. Two boys, clearly brothers, hopped up on chocolate ice cream, with brown smears around their mouths, collided with her as she came through the door. The larger one stepped square on her foot.

The boys' mother, paying her check at the cashier, hadn't witnessed the incident. The boys did not apologize. They merely ducked around her and out the door.

"That's okay," Sara muttered to herself. "I've got other toes. I'll manage." She limped to the hostess station. "Hi. I'm meeting a friend, but I don't know if he's here yet. He's tall...blonde..."

"Oh, you mean Johnny!" The teenage hostess, black hair tied up high in a ponytail, flashed Sara a friendly smile. "Sure, he's here. Through that door on the left, booth on the right side."

"Thanks." Sara felt a strange twinge of jealousy. The cute little hostess knew Johnny by name. *Isn't that sweet?* She wondered just how many cuties in how many restaurants knew Johnny by name. Waitresses, cashiers, hostesses—it could add up to quite a little harem.

She felt a flutter of panic in her throat. Was she developing feelings for Johnny? And if so, how could she compete with all the sweet young things around town?

"Sara!"

Entering the small dining room, she saw Johnny's hand raised in greeting. His welcoming smile melted her worries away.

"Hi!" She slid in across from him, wriggling off her lightweight jacket and pushing it with her purse to the other end of the bench. " I have a question."

"Shoot."

"Whatever happened to the adage, 'early to bed, early to rise?' Why are children eating dinner at this hour? When I was their age, I was already in bed." Sara was venting her frustration caused by the throbbing of her big toe.

"That's two questions, Mrs. Goode, and aren't you sexy when you revert to your teacher mode."

"If you like that," she quipped in her Mae West imitation," You should come and see me when I have bus duty. I'm a regular sexpot."

Johnny laughed, all the crinkles around his eyes and mouth working together.

"Did you order?" she asked.

"Without you? What do you think I am, a heathen?"

"Well, I don't know. You might have ordered if you were hungry enough. Besides, it isn't like this is a date or anything, right?" Sara wanted Johnny to like her, even flirt a little with her, but she had her line drawn in the sand. She'd been burned, and she had to keep away from the fire.

Johnny shook his head. "Would it be so terrible if it was a date? A date between two very good friends?"

Sara looked Johnny straight in the eye, trying to decide if he was pressuring her. She decided to leave well enough alone. "I guess not," she sighed.

"Anyway, I have some bad news to tell you," said Johnny.

Fear gripped her. Possibilities filled her mind. The worst? He was going to move somewhere far away, and she would be left without her ardent admirer.

"Our waitress," said Johnny portentously, "is a bubblehead."

Relieved, she asked, "Don't you mean 'bobble?'" She hadn't seen the waitress yet, but the hostess certainly looked like something adorable you'd find on the shelf of a gift shop.

"Nope. I mean 'bubble.' A certifiable nut."

"Why?"

"Look around the room. What do you see?"

Sara discreetly surveyed the other booth. One was empty, dirty dishes remaining from the previous customers. One held middle-aged couple with a teen-aged boy. The rest were clean and empty.

"Slow night at the Eat 'n Park?" Sara wondered.

Johnny's wiggled his eyebrows in a villainous way.

"Didn't we talk about the eyebrow thing?" Sara said.

"Yes, yes," he said. "But you still haven't solved my puzzle, gorgeous."

"You're such a flirt today, Johnny Boy. What's gotten into you?"

"Must be spring fever. But since you're stumped, I'll tell you." He leaned across the table and whispered. "There's no food or drink on any of the tables, including ours."

"Huh. What's up with that?" Eat 'n Park usually had fast service. The waitresses attended closely to their tables, refilling water glasses, dropping hot rolls into the bread basket and suggesting their famous strawberry pie for dessert.

"Where *is* the waitress?" Sara peered towards the kitchen and reception area. "Do you think one of us should go and look for her?"

"I'm telling you, Sara, she's nuts. She took the orders at that other table about ten minutes ago, and she hasn't been back since. It's the most mind-boggling disappearance since Amelia Earhart's!"

Sara laughed out loud. "A dingo ate my waitress!" she said, stealing a line from her favorite '90s sitcom.

Johnny's eyes lit up. "'No soup for you!'"

Sara couldn't leave well enough alone. She cried out, "No soup for anyone!"

The family next to them looked up. The father smiled wearily.

"Well done." Johnny quickly reached across the table and grabbed Sara's hand. "Shh! Here she comes."

The waitress, a throwback from the '50s with impossibly tall hair and pink bubble gum cracking in her mouth, appeared at the end of their booth. "Hi. Would you like to order something to drink?" She didn't make eye contact with them, but stood with her pencil poised over her pad.

Johnny gestured to Sara. "Ladies first."

"I'll have a diet pop," she said.

"Would that be Pepsi or Coke?"

"Um, I guess I'll take Pepsi."

"Sorry, we only have Coke."

Sara swallowed a burst of laughter. Johnny was right—they were in the presence of a real Pittsburgh bubblehead. Either that, or the waitress had been born too close to one of the long-gone steel mills on the banks of the Monongahela River.

"Then," Sara said in her kindergarten teacher voice, slow as to not be mistaken, "I'll take the Coke."

"Sure," the waitress scribbled something down on her pad. "And for the gentleman?"

Johnny winked at Sara. "I'll have a black coffee. No milk, no sugar, just the goodness of the coffee bean."

The waitress stuck the pen up in her hair. "I know what black coffee means."

Johnny nodded thoughtfully. "Yes, I guess you would."

Sara added, "He was just waxing poetic."

The waitress gave Johnny a long stare. "The only thing waxed around here are my legs, so I'd appreciate it if you'd leave the fancy talk for your girlfriend and let me get back to business."

Johnny pretended to zip his lips closed and throw away an imaginary key. The waitress stalked away.

"I'm not getting my coffee, am I?"

Sara settled back, enjoying the simple, quiet companionship of an old friend. She looked up when she realized that Johnny was staring at her.

"How's it going with your Bat Buddy, Adam West?"

"I sent the letter a few days ago, just like we talked about. Of course I haven't heard anything back yet." Sara cupped her head in her hands. "I have a feeling that I'm not going to get a reply. If you think about it, he's got millions of fans all around the world. Why would he answer my little letter?"

"Be a shame if he didn't. I know how much it means to you to make a connection,"

"It would be nice." Sara looked up and saw the waitress approaching their table with a glass of soda. She placed it on the table in front of Sara without saying a word then walked out of the room.

"See? No coffee."

Sara took a long sip from her glass. It was Coke all right, but it wasn't diet. At that point Sara didn't care. She was happy to have something, anything, to fill her stomach. "Aaahhh," she exhaled in complete satisfaction. "They're right: Coke is it."

"I have an idea,"

"I'm not sharing this Coke with you. I like you and everything, but I'm starving and I want this soda all for myself."

"No, no. I'm talking about Adam West, not the soda," said Johnny.

"Okay, then, out with it."

"I was poking around the web and discovered that Adam is going to be at a media convention in Toronto next weekend."

Sara stopped slurping her drink. "Next weekend? Isn't Toronto far from here?"

"Yes, next weekend. And it's six hours by car."

"You'd drive six hours with me so that I could see Adam West in person?"

"Well, not me, exactly, since I have to work the weekend," said Johnny. "But I did get someone near and dear to you to volunteer for the trip."

"Oh?" Sara asked warily. "And who might that be?"

"Joe Norris."

Sara was incredulous. "Joe said that he would like to sit in a car with me for six straight hours and attend a nerdy fan convention in Toronto?'

"I offered him an incentive," Johnny said. "I told him I'd redo the cabinets in his kitchen for a once-in-a-lifetime, low, low rate."

"How low?" Sara asked.

"Free."

"Johnny! That's crazy!"

Johnny's accustomed bravado vanished. He said tenderly, "Not for something that will make you happy."

"Oh, Johnny. I don't think…" She felt the pressure that she always experienced when Johnny went out of his way to please her.

"That's right. You don't think, you just go and enjoy. There are no strings attached to this offer. I know what it would mean for you to meet Adam West in person, so I'm giving you the opportunity. Go and have fun."

"You are an incredible friend, Johnny."

"Just remember that I care, Sara. We've both been through a lot lately, and we deserve to do things that will feed our soul."

"So what are you going to do to 'feed your soul?'" Sara asked.

"Getting your wise-cracking self out of this town should suffice." Johnny smirked at her. He was a rascal, but he was undeniably *her* rascal.

"Uh-oh. Who's going to take care of Dog while I'm gone?"

"I can handle him for the weekend. I have some neighbor boys that can play with him while I'm at work. It should be no problem," Johnny said.

The waitress returned to their table with a carafe of coffee. "More coffee?" she asked Johnny.

Johnny looked down at the empty table in front of him, then back up at Sara. "And would you take Bubbles with you?"

CHAPTER EIGHT

"Get in the left lane, Sara. You can pass that guy now," Joe said impatiently. He was getting on Sara's last nerve. "Now. Do it now!"

Sara ignored Joe and stayed within drafting distance of the semi in front of her Mini Cooper.

"Well, you just lost that window of opportunity. " Joe flopped back in his seat with a resigned sigh. Joe could give whatever orders he wanted; Sara would never have passed the truck. It would have meant speeding on a Canadian highway, which she had no intention of doing. Sara knew they were going to be late getting to Toronto, but she had no interest in breaking laws in a foreign country. It was Friday, a week after Johnny had suggested this trip. They had hotel two rooms booked, then it would be over to the convention center in the morning to see Adam West.

"What's our ETA?" Sara asked Joe to halt his cursing of the planet-sized truck in front of them.

"Well, you've blown my original projections by being so stingy on the pedal. In a few miles, we're going to be stuck in Canadian rush hour. And from what I've heard, it's a hell that I shouldn't have to experience even once in a lifetime." Joe's rant that caused him to lift his chin higher so that he had to look down his nose at Sara.

"What could you possibly know about Canadian highways?"

"I have my sources. Google much, honey? You are going to be so sorry that you said you would drive the second half of the trip."

Sara had worked the morning at school and had managed to find a sub for the afternoon. Joe drove the first leg of the journey as Sara had unwound from a hectic few hours with her kindergarteners. Now Sara was stuck driving the tedious part.

Sara shrugged, swigged a mouthful of diet cola from the plastic bottle in her cup holder and kept her eyes on the backside of the truck ahead. The semi's bumper sticker read, "This vehicle eats compact cars for breakfast." In response, Sara lightened the pressure of her foot on the accelerator and put some distance between her car and certain death.

Joe clicked his tongue at her with impatience. His arrival time projections were just blown out of the water. It reminded Sara of the time she was traveling in Florida at Christmas with her parents. As their car sped down the highway, with the interior heated to 80 degrees, Sara cracked a window to gulp in a badly needed breath of fresh air. Dad turned around in his seat and barked, "Close that window. It's cutting down on our aerodynamics." It was all Sara could do to keep from laughing out loud then, and that's exactly how she felt sitting next to the tightly wound Joe Norris. She needed to change tactics before she totally lost it with him.

"Joe," Sara sweetly said, "Have I thanked you for being such a good buddy and coming along on this trip with me?"

"Not in the last hour, but you're welcome. It really would have been a long trip for you to do on your own."

Sara nodded her agreement, "Little did I know that I would be making this whirlwind trip to Toronto. I..."

Joe screamed, interrupting her. "What in hell?"

The semi in front of them had careened abruptly into the left lane. No more than a half mile in front of them, in their lane, sat an opened lawn chair facing in the opposite direction. Cars wildly swerved to the left or right, avoiding both the chair and the other cars that were clearing the lane.

"Someone is sitting in the chair!" Sara yelled. She uttered a few curses, then pulled hard to the right, managing to squeeze tightly between two SUVs. She thanked her lucky stars that she was driving one of the smallest cars on earth. She grabbed at her chest while trying to catch her breath from the shock. As she applied the brakes and slowly drove by the lawn chair, both she and Joe craned their heads to take a look.

"Oh, for the love of Pete!" said Joe. Attached to the top of the chair was a stuffed bear fluttering in the wind caused by passing cars.

"Thank goodness!" Sara exclaimed. "I swear that it looked like someone was sitting in the chair."

"I know! But it's still a hazard. Someone could run right into that chair and damage their car pretty badly. Or get killed trying to avoid hitting it."

"I wish we could stop," Sara said, "and clear the chair off the road, but traffic's moving too fast. It must have fallen off an open truck or the top of a car."

"When we get to the hotel, I'm going to need a drink," Joe said. "We're getting into Toronto way behind schedule, and it didn't help my nerves to have some random lawn chair sitting in the middle of the highway." He turned for one last look behind then faced Sara. "Hey, honeybuns, that was some slick maneuvering you did back there. Thanks for saving my life. You were like a superhero."

"Like a Gal Wonder?" Sara reminded Joe of the nickname he had given her last week.

Joe smiled and said, "Just like a Gal Wonder."

"Well, it's the least I could do, keeping you out of danger. Not everyone would have traveled all the way to Canada just so their friend could meet a childhood idol." Sara's eyes filled with tears. Was it gratitude, or the knowledge that they had escaped death by lawn chair and teddy bear just moments before?

"I'm cool with this trip, Sara. It gets me out of the list of chores my mother had lined up for me at her place this weekend. And Johnny's kitchen renovation for my apartment is a sweet incentive; I won't deny that," Joe said.

"Well, despite the fact that you're getting a new kitchen out of this, I think you're a kind man. So, when is Johnny going to find the time to work on your cabinets? He's really wrapped up with that Waterfront project."

"I can be patient," Joe said, a response to which Sara had to bite her tongue. "No rush. Besides, I'm busy myself, what with my job and then helping to find the elementary school hacker."

"Yeah, how's that going? I don't hear much of the scuttlebutt, now that Jen is working overtime and missing lunches and happy hours." Sara hadn't seen Jen in over a week, which was highly unusual for a member of their tight group.

"We're getting closer to figuring this out. We've set up an Internet trap, so that when the culprit attempts to hack in again, we're going to be able to grab his on-line signature and identify our man—or... child, as the case may be." Joe sounded excited.

"I guess you and Jen are spending lots of time together on this, aren't you?"

"No more than the situation warrants." Joe's response was so awkwardly formal that Sara glanced at him in surprise. His face was flushed a bright red from forehead to neck. Something was up, no doubt about it.

"Why, Joe Norris. I don't think I've ever seen you blush. What could be the source of this discomfort?" She so rarely got to tease Joe about *his* potential love life, so no way was she going to be subtle. Besides, five hours in a car with his bossiness left her wanting to get one up on him.

Joe was having none of it. "Back off, Goode."

"I don't think so, Norris. What's going on?"

"Nothing that you need to know about." Joe's body had become rigid, and Sara could see his neck veins pulsing.

"Now, Joe, it's just you and me, sitting alone in this car, with traffic jams ahead and Pittsburgh miles behind us. You are my prisoner in this vehicle, so you should feel a certain, um, responsibility to share any interesting information with me," Sara said.

"Sara, do I needle you about everything you say and do with Johnny?"

"Why, yes, you do. Quite often, as a matter of fact."

Joe looked away from her, out the passenger window. The scenery had abruptly transitioned from the fresh woods of springtime to the factories and warehouses of Canada.

"Let's make a deal," Joe said.

"Intriguing. Go on." Sara figured she had nothing to lose and all the juicy information about this new romance to gain.

"How about this? I'll tell you a little something about my *alleged* situation with Jen if you answer a question of mine."

"One question only," Sara said. It's not that she didn't trust Joe, but in love and war, she never knew what he might try to get away with.

"Sure, one question, I promise." Joe sounded sincere, but Sara knew his one question was going to be tough. Joe could bring up her divorce, her age, her lack of male companionship, her Adam West quest, her lack of fashion sense, her extra pounds...*Oh, hell,* she thought, *there isn't much else to do for the next hour.* As Joe had predicted, they were stuck in a bumper-to-bumper, king-size Canadian traffic jam.

"Okay, Cubby. Hit me with your best shot." Sara stared at the offensive message written with a finger in the dust of another truck that had slipped into the lane in front of her Mini Cooper.

Joe turned in his seat and faced Sara directly. "Why can't you admit that you have feelings for Johnny?"

"Feelings? Not again, Joe! Johnny is not the love of my life. Why can't you just accept that I'm not going to let it become anything more than a friendship?" Sara asked.

"Why can't you accept that you care about him as more than a friend? You're clearly denying yourself the opportunity to explore what's out there."

"Oh, Joe. It's not that easy. In fact, it's impossible."

"Sara, it is *that* easy. All you have to do is open that door and walk through it." Joe pantomimed opening a door, then whooshed his hands forward as if moving in the direction she should take. "Just walk through."

"So sayeth the man who hasn't had a girlfriend in years," said Sara.

"We're not talking about me, Sara. That's so typical of you, trying to change the subject." Joe cocked his head towards Sara, his eyes glinting with mild amusement. "Tell me, Sara, what are you afraid of?"

Sara gripped the steering wheel tightly, even though the car was stopped dead in the parking lot that the expressway had become. "Okay, this is the story, once and for all." Sara took a deep breath to clear her thoughts. "I can't let myself feel anything for a man who has shown that he is capable of throwing away my love. A long time ago, I gave Johnny my heart. And what did he do? He treated my feelings as if they were garbage. It hurt so bad I thought I would die. But I got over it. I was doing okay until I married a man who used my heart for target practice. There's a theme running through my relationships, Joe. Any time I care deeply about someone, they turn around and hurt me." Sara slammed the palm of her hand on the steering wheel for emphasis. "I will never, ever let anyone do that to me again."

Joe was silent for a few moments, digesting her words. "Oh, Sara. What happened between you and Johnny took place a long time ago. You and Johnny have each lived a lifetime since then. You're adults now. You're not the same people you were in high school. Sure, Johnny acted like a jerk back then. And sure, you deserved to be angry at him. But what is the statute of limitations on holding a grudge? What happened in your marriage has absolutely nothing to do with Johnny. Grow up, Sara. Let the pain of the past go, and allow yourself some happiness. Johnny is perfect for you. In fact, both of you are perfect for each other. Don't let your stubbornness be the one barrier to what could be a lifetime of happiness."

Sara could feel her eyes widening in shock. "Wow." She cleared her throat. "Since when did you become such an expert on relationships?"

"If you're trying to hurt me with that comment, Sara, it won't work. I've needed to tell you this for a while, and you gave me the perfect opening."

"Lucky me. Now I'm the prisoner in this car."

"And while we're on the subject of you, I'd like to share some things I've learned about you over the last few months. I think you need to hear this." Joe twisted to face her more directly.

Sara felt a bit cold inside as her feelings started shutting down. She guessed that this numbness would get her through whatever Joe was going to dish out next.

"Okay," she said quietly.

"Here are the facts about Sara Goode, as seen by Joe Norris. Number One, you think that you know everything about yourself, but, in fact, you do not. Number Two, you think that your sense of humor hides your true feelings about things. It does not, although anyone who knows you enjoys your ability to laugh at yourself. And Number Three, you think that that Johnny will always be there as your default guy, the one man who will spend his life putting you on that pedestal you're so fond of, but he will not. Someday, he's going to get tired of waiting for you, and he's going to move on. He's a normal, warm-blooded man who needs to give his love to some equally warm and affectionate woman." As he finished, Joe turned away. "You don't want to be stuck with some weird burning man, do you?"

With the car still stopped, and no sign of movement ahead, Sara rested her forehead on the steering wheel.

"So you know about Burning Man," she said after a few moments. "It figures that Jen couldn't keep it a secret. She just had to tell you, Mr. Up-in-Everybody's-Business. So what else am I doing wrong, Joe?"

"Sara, I'm not criticizing you. I told you, I'm sharing my observations. If you think I'm just listing your faults, then maybe you need to take a long look at yourself."

Sara lifted her head and smiled. "I'm rubber, you're glue, what you say bounces off me and sticks to you."

"Uhhhh... Very mature?"

"Mature?" Sara could hear the hysteria rising in her voice. "You're sitting with me in a car bound for Toronto so that I can meet the superhero of my past, and you dare bring maturity into this? I'm not mature, Joe. I'm a freak of nature. I want to meet Batman. What makes you think I can make sane decisions about anything else in my life based on this fact? I'll tell you what, let's get through this weekend, and then maybe I'll consider facing your so-called facts about me."

"Fair enough." Joe actually looked apologetic. "Okay. Just calm down. We'll talk about it later." He breathed in deeply then exhaled in a loud rush. "Would you like to hear about me and Jen?"

"I think I've earned the right to that information," Sara said.

"So...Jen and I are both putting our feelers out. We've had some long conversations that have led me to believe that she could be as interested in me as I am in her. I think we'll probably take this to the next level, once the whole computer scam is solved. Right now, we're being professional and keeping our distance. But, I think this could develop into something meaningful."

"And you have the audacity to say that I'm not pursuing my feelings?" Sara began to laugh.

"Do as I say, Sara, not as I do," Joe said. "But, seriously, I fully intend to explore this connection between Jen and me. You can take that to the bank, as they say."

"Do they also say that you're a geek?" Sara asked.

"A loveable geek, I'd like to think," Joe said.

"I hope Jen knows what she's getting into," said Sara. "Hey, do those buildings in the distance mean we're getting close to Toronto?"

"I do believe it's the Emerald City, dear Dorothy. Or should I say, Gotham City?" Joe winked.

Sara stared at the Toronto skyline. "Holy road trip from hell, it looks like I'm going to get to meet Adam West after all."

CHAPTER NINE

"Alrighty…this looks like the line."

Sara had glimpsed Adam West from afar. He was seated at a table, signing photos, shaking hands and letting fans grab candid photos and selfies with him. She took a moment to control the wild beating of her heart, then had to take more than a few moments to find the end of Adam's autograph line. She needed to join that line immediately, before she lost her courage and ran out of the hall and all the way back to Pittsburgh.

Sara and Joe trailed along the dozens awaiting a chance to gape at their favorite superhero, up close and personal. They were talking loudly, laughing loudly, even breathing loudly. Sara felt her nerves lighting up like spark plugs.

"No, wait, it goes around this corner." Sara discovered that the line actually took a sharp right turn around a corner, and an additional hundred or so autograph seekers streamed from there to the back of the convention hall.

"Oh, lord," Joe moaned. "We'll be here till Christmas. And I've been such a good boy this year. Thank heavens we stopped for Starbucks." He sipped his venti caramel latte, breathed a sigh of satisfaction. "I can't believe you didn't get one."

"My nerves are shot as it is," Sara said as she pulled Joe gently-but-firmly by the sleeve of his tee shirt to the dark recesses of the hall. They joined the line behind a gourd-shaped, myopic gentleman who was wearing hipster glasses (non-ironically) and a faded Batman-logo T-shirt. His age was indeterminate; he could have been fifty, or he could have been eighteen. He seemed friendly enough, but when he made direct eye contact with Sara, he asked, in a halting drone, "Are you aware that the autograph is fifty dollars? Another ten for a photo."

Sara gulped. "Well, no, I wasn't, but I guess it doesn't matter. I didn't drive six hours to let the cost of the autograph ruin my chance to meet Adam West."

Myopic Guy stared at her, unblinking. Behind his glasses, his eyes looked about five time normal human size. "I thought you should know."

Sara gave a tight, polite smile. "Well, thanks." She began to turn to Joe, but apparently The Master of Myopia wasn't done with her.

"They don't have the price posted, and some people have had a nasty surprise." Then he actually blinked three times in rapid succession.

Sara gave the barest "mm-hmm," hoping to end the conversation. No luck with that.

"One lady waited a full hour before she heard the cost, and she had to leave the line because she didn't have enough money with her. She used some bad words, and threw a Danish at Security."

The guy was obviously rattled by the high price. Sara felt like suggesting he should leave the line if it bothered him so much. "Listen, buddy, I already said that I'm fine with the price. Can we just leave it at that?"

He stared myopically again. He opened his mouth then quickly shut it, reminding Sara of her goldfish, Goldie, and her hopes that Nicole would remember to feed the fish during her weekend away. Sara turned a triumphant smile in Joe's direction, but he had developed a keen interest in the glossy convention program book.

"I just thought you should know." Myopic Guy said. Did this guy just have to have the last word? Sara whipped around and held her pointer finger stiffly in front of his eyes to silence him. "That's it. No more. Hush yourself." The abashed geek sniffed loudly, then blessedly did an about-face.

Sara rested her head on Joe's shoulder. "Save me, Joe."

"Save yourself, wench. It's every man, woman and geek for themselves. And I'm going to let you choose which category you fit in." He flipped to another a page in the program. "Oh, my, god! Summer Glau is here! From *Firefly*!"

"I see. So who's the geek now, Joe Norris?"

Joe closed the program book and tucked it under his arm. "I'm the geek. I've got to go and see her. I'll be right back." Joe slipped away before Sara could grab his collar. His royal blue shirt disappeared into the crowd and the horror of the situation sunk in immediately. She was alone in line to see her childhood idol, with no one to support her and stop her from running away like a wild child.

"Please come back, Joe," Sara whispered.

Myopic Guy turned and said, "Guess he didn't want to pay the fifty dollars."

Sara ignored him and studied the other fans around her. Most seemed normal enough—high school couples holding hands, wannabe frat boys laughing at nothing, a swarm of Goth teens, twin boys with their dad. Most seemed excited to be here, allowing Sara to relax. *Okay,* she said to herself, *I can do this. It's no big deal; I'm just another fan getting an autograph and sharing a few words with an actor.*

Who's just a person.

A person I've adored since I was —

Oh my God, that's Adam-freaking-West!

Sara physically stiffened her spine to suppress an urge to cut and run. *Just a person,* she reminded herself again.

Sara was pretty sure that Adam would be easy to talk with. Heaven knows he was easy to look at, both then and now. From her vantage point, she could see him through the curtain that hung behind his booth. Sara studied Adam's profile as he greeted each new fan and signed the glossy Batman photos his manager was selling. Manager or assistant? He was a middle-aged, surfer-dude type. Adam wore a casual white button-down cotton shirt and blue jeans. His hair was thinning, but he had golden highlights to accent his buttery brown tan. He was in terrific shape, not an ounce of fat on his long frame. That Sara could see, anyway. He sat in a folding chair with his legs stretching far under the tablecloth. His shoulders were still broad; the breadth of his chest under his shirt suggested smooth contours over muscles that had withstood the test of time.

Adam was definitely older. Of course, everyone shows some effects of aging eventually, but she could clearly see that he was still the Adam West of her youth in his gamut of facial expressions. He had a quick smile with soft lips, and his eyes crinkled in the corners with warmth and humor. Sara could have watched him all day from relative obscurity behind the curtain, but a hand suddenly drew the curtain shut while a voice yelled, "No peeking behind the curtains! Do that again and you'll be expelled from the convention!"

The curtain folds closed on Sara's view of Adam. A heavyset woman wearing a convention logo tee shirt glared at Sara with her arms crossed sternly across her ample breasts.

Sara knew she should have said, *Wow, study customer service much?* Sadly, she was so frightened by the threat that she might miss meeting Adam West after all those miles—and all these years—that she just babbled:

"Oh, yes, ma'am. I mean, no, ma'am. I won't do it again. I promise." She blushed furiously at getting caught in her voyeuristic enjoyment and scolded like one of her kindergartners. Thank goodness the she-witch had closed the curtain before Adam could turn around to check on the disturbance behind him. That one small mercy made it possible for Sara to meet the stares of the people around her with a chagrined smile. Even Myopic Guy snickered. If the security person hadn't still been looking at Sara with her evil eyes, she'd have put the bastard in a headlock so fast he wouldn't have been able to remember the serial number of the starship *Enterprise*. Sara was a stranger in a strange land. She certainly wasn't Cinderella at the ball, as Joe had suggested. Oh, no. She was Alice, endlessly falling down the rabbit hole.

Sara looked hopefully for Joe, but he had long ago vanished into the swirling crowds. The convention had many other actor guests to draw the fannish sorts, as well as tables filled with television and movie memorabilia for sale and special areas where the latest and greatest video games could be tried out for future purchase consideration. Sara focused on keeping a low profile and practicing her speech for Adam West. It had to be perfect so that she could show Adam how much his Batman meant to her.

First, Sara figured, she'd say hello in a sincere, from-the-heart manner while making direct contact with his gorgeous eyes. She would choose a photograph for him to sign, preferably one that was more recent than those publicity stills from the Sixties. Choosing a current photo might give him the idea that it was Adam West, the actor and the man, she'd come to see, and not the make-believe superhero that had fought the villains of Gotham City.

As Adam was signing the photo, she'd tell him that he was a guiding influence in her life and that she wouldn't be the successful woman she was today without his television character to challenge her imagination, just as she had written in the letter that he obviously had never received. Sara would name some of the shows she'd seen him in over the last few months, and then tell him how glad she was that his career had been rejuvenated as a new generation discovered his comedic talents. Then she would reach her left hand across the table to accept her signed picture while extending her right hand to shake his hand. At this point Sara would smile sweetly and tell Adam West that he would always be her idol.

Yes, that should do it. She would finally be able to say thank-you to him directly and know that he had received her message. She would finally be free of the nagging, incomplete feeling that she'd carried ever since she viewed the *Return to the Batcave* movie with Joe. Sara's quest would come to an end with this one, bittersweet meeting.

The import of this moment made Sara's thoughts swirl and caused her head to ache. It seemed unreal, her standing there just a few feet from Adam West. It wasn't every day that you got to meet your childhood hero.

But why was she there, really and truly? If she searched within herself, could she honestly say that Adam's superhero alter ego had been so influential? Sara knew that, at thirteen, a girl like her could be impressionable as she fought to carve out her own identity. She knew boys at that age who had been nuts about "their" football team and would memorize all the stats for their favorite players. Sara supposed that, in the same way, she had idolized Adam West in his roles of Bruce Wayne and Batman.

There was definitely the male/female thing, the attraction she felt to the strapping young man in the mysterious costume and the girlish crush she suffered every time Bruce Wayne made an appearance in stately Wayne Manor. That attraction was a given, and Sara was certainly one among the millions who felt it. Of course, she was also affected by the actor himself, his deep voice, his studied mannerisms, and his penetrating eyes.

Batman transported her twice weekly from the daily aches and pains of adolescence to a place of exciting make-believe. She was as angst-ridden as any other child of the baby boomer generation, and Batman was the embodiment of all good things. He could lift Sara away from the family room's slippery Naugahyde couch to the cool, safe confines of the Batcave. There she could explore the powers that would transform her from a child into a woman.

She had identified with the sleek lines of the Batmobile, the shiny, rich folds of the silken capes, and the thoughtful, steepled fingers of Batman as he brainstormed with Commissioner Gordon. It was a vibrant world, alive with creativity and stimulating to Sara's young mind—with Adam West at its center. He was the man who made it all come alive. And he must be acknowledged. Adam was the reason that Sara stood in this wacky autograph line that was moving ever so slowly forward.

Yes, indeed, she needed to thank Adam West.

It seemed almost miraculous to Sara that she was going to be speaking to him now, to be meeting her past right here and now. She would be a stranger to him, yet she knew so much about his life. Maybe he *had* never received her letter, but he would soon know its contents from her own lips. For Sara, it would be closure.

It didn't look like Joe was going to return in time to share this historic moment. Sara could do nothing but keep breathing deeply, in and out, in and out, to try and stay calm and in control of her nerves. She told herself that it wasn't only fear making her body tremble, it was excitement as well. Sara hadn't felt this rush of pleasure and pain since she'd opened her front door and seen Johnny in the hallway holding a bouquet of wildflowers the day after she had moved back to her hometown.

Adam West was now only feet away from Sara. There were only two people to go before she had her chance to speak with him. Suddenly, the hour wait, which had been boring and mind-numbing, seemed too short. Sara needed more time to pull her thoughts together, to rehearse her speech one last time.

Her hands became cold and clammy. She rubbed them on the hem of her beige lace top, then on her short, light blue denim skirt. Was this an appropriate outfit for meeting this famous man? Did it look like she was trying to be younger than she really was? Did she look like all the other fans in line, trying hard to make an impression and failing miserably?

Now only Myopic Guy and one other fan stood between Sara and Adam. They both watched the former caped crusader smiled beneficently at the fan in front of them, as a liege might graciously smile on a supplicant. Adam was signing an infamous photo of himself as Batman, carrying a bomb with a lit fuse over his head. What was the funny line from the 1966 *Batman* movie? She couldn't think, and thus she couldn't remember.

Now Myopic Guy was stepping forward, and Sara was the cheese, standing all alone at the front of the autograph line. It was like waiting in line for Santa Claus when you're about six or seven years old. You didn't actually want to meet the guy because he was so powerful, so big, so important to you, but you sure wanted him to know that you were expecting a baby doll under the tree on Christmas morning.

Sara softly cleared her throat several times, licked her lips and tried to pull a smile out of her frozen facial muscles. She wasn't meeting Mother Theresa or even the President of the United States; it was Adam West, for goodness sakes. It was Batman.

Yeah. That was scarier than all the others put together.

It was her turn.

Sara stood rooted to her spot for a few seconds as Adam and his manager whispered something to each other. She looked at Adam, only three feet away from her, and experienced the most incredible out-of-body feeling. She was there, and yet, she wasn't. Adam's manager signaled her to step forward. Sara handed him her money and scanned the photos to make a choice. Somehow, a black and white photo of Batman in full costume was in her hands, and Sara was sliding it on the table towards Adam. Adam looked at her with his eyebrows slightly raised. "Name?" he asked.

Sara panicked. What did he mean, name? "Pardon me?"

"Who would you like me to make this out to?" Adam's eyes softened kindly at her confusion.

"Me, mine, uh...*Sara!*" Had she never spoken before? No one would believe that she had passed the teaching exams in the top percentile.

"S-a-r-a-h?" Adam recited the traditional spelling of her name.

"No, without the 'h,' please." She leaned into the table and watched as he wrote her name in a legible and sweeping script. Her simple name had never looked so grand. Sara didn't want this moment to end. She could stand there forever, watching Adam's large hand with his diamond ring on his middle finger as he wrote her name.

Adam signed his own name then looked up at Sara. He smiled sweetly. "There you go." He pushed the photograph across the table towards her.

Sara shot a smile back at him. "Adam, I want to thank you…" She paused as she tried to remember the words to her carefully designed speech. "Thank you…," she said again.

His smile was dazzling. His voice was warm. "You're quite welcome," And then, no doubt thinking that Sara had completed what she wanted to say, he turned to the next person in line.

Sara stayed put, wanting to say all the words that would let him know what he meant to her, yet finding nothing coming out. She slowly stepped to the side as the next fan handed Adam a photo. "Leonard," he said, and Adam picked up his pen.

Sara walked, looking backwards. It couldn't be. Her moment was over before it had begun. It was a classic case of stage fright. Adam was still there, looking cool and reserved, while Sara stood on the fringes of the crowd, flustered and confused. Without a doubt… she had blown it.

CHAPTER TEN

"What a kick in the pants," Sara said aloud to herself. She was standing ten feet from her childhood idol, the one and only Batman, and all she had to show for 50 bucks and an hour in the autograph line was, well... an autograph. And a sense of bewilderment. Oh, yes, and a black and white photo of Adam in a superhero stance.

"Wow," she muttered. There sat Adam West, smiling, signing, being glib with fans. And there she stood, staring, muttering, gawking. Was "gawking" a thing? It must be. She was a gawky, awkward fan—a fan who wanted Adam's attention for just a few moments so she could reveal her deepest feelings. So she could let him know he was still *mattered*. To her.

And she would never get the chance again.

She had gotten her big chance, and she had let it slip by her like a puff of smoke in the wind.

Joe chose that moment to reappear at Sara's side.

"Hey, Princess! How'd it go?" Yep, there he was. Happy smile. Bright eyes. She wanted to throttle him.

"It was, um, *weird*."

"Weird, huh? Yeah, those movie star types can be strange."

"No, Adam wasn't weird. *I* was weird," said Sara.

Joe grimaced, no doubt trying to think of something to say that wouldn't get him poked in the chest or left with one tee shirt sleeve longer than the other. She had to admit she was pretty rough on the poor guy.

For no reason she could fathom, Sara laughed. The pain of her abortive meeting with Adam West was settling in her stomach and threatening to burn out her intestines, but... she laughed. Joe never knew the right thing to say. He was bossy. He was nerdy. He was hopeless.

Right then she loved him more than anyone in the world.

She looped her arm through his. "Let's get something to eat, and I'll tell you the whole, pathetic story."

Across the convention floor was a concession stand that sold pizza, hot dogs, meatball sandwiches, and cookies—the usual convention center heart attack chow. Sara pushed a tray along the cold metal counter and gathered a donut with chocolate frosting, an over-sized chocolate chip cookie and a large Coke, no ice. Joe, clearly more health-conscious, chose a hot dog and chips.

As she paid the cashier ("Velma," the lady's nametag read) Sara spotted a basket of candy bars by the register. "Wait!" she cried, and grabbed a large Butterfinger.

Velma rolled her eyes. "Will that be all?"

Sarcasm? Wondered Sara. she met Velma's eyes. *Yes. Sarcasm. Definitely sarcasm.*

Sara felt her body stiffen in the way it did when she had been insulted, knew it, and she was about to respond in kind. Behind her, she heard Joe mutter, "Oh, no."

"Well, no, I don't think that *is* all."

Sara grabbed a few Snickers bars, a few Milky Ways and some M&M's, and heaped them on her tray. Deciding there was not enough sugar there to ensure a diabetic coma, she grabbed two more handfuls from the basket. "There," Sara said. "I guess that'll do it." She arched an eyebrow at Velma. "Problem?"

Sara hoped that her expression conveyed the message that any problem would push her over the edge of crazy into raving lunatic.

Velma's eyes widened. She rang up the food without blinking. "The total comes to $25.50," she said.

Sara coughed into her hand and muttered some choice words about the high cost of junk food. She fumbled in her wallet for the money, searching among her ATM receipts, bubblegum wrappers and grocery store coupons. She found a few dollar bills, but she couldn't seem to find the extra twenty-dollar bill she'd slid into her wallet that morning. With a jolt, she remembered. Adam West's autograph had been fifty dollars, and not the twenty-five or thirty she had expected it would be based on her research on the Internet. She looked up at Velma in blind panic.

Suddenly, Joe's hand swept past Sara, filled with dollar bills. "This should cover both our orders." Joe nudged Sara with his tray. "Come on, sugar baby, let's go find a table."

Finding a table and sitting, Sara smiled sheepishly at Joe, "Thanks."

"What 'thanks?' You owe me Goode."

Sara groaned at his little joke on her name.

"I know." Sara started to slip her autographed photo on to the table, but then held it up for Joe to see. "Cool, huh?"

"Sure. Mr. West has great handwriting. But why did you pick black and white?" Joe took a chomp out of his hotdog and handed the picture back to Sara.

"Exactly. Why didn't I pick a color picture? Why didn't I do anything that I had planned on doing?" Sara asked.

"Didn't you get to thank him?" Joe asked, amazed.

"That's all I did. I said ' thank you.' No speech, no tribute, no meaningful anything. I merely said 'thank you.'"

"That's it?"

"Yes. Well, actually, I said it twice. 'Thank you' and 'thank you.'"

Joe continued to stare at Sara, his hot dog held in mid-air and dripping mustard down on his chip bag. "You're a goof."

"Yes, I'm a goof."

"Huh." Joe put his hot dog down and reached over to Sara's plate to snag a granola bar that had somehow become part of the mix. She had already scarfed down the donut and was working with precision on the chocolate chip cookie.

"Want to see my Summer Glau picture?" Joe asked.

"Sure, why not?" said Sara.

Sara took the color photo of Summer and read the inscription. *To Joe. Love, Summer Glau.*

"Well, aren't you the lucky one? 'Love, Summer Glau?' All I got was 'To Sara, Adam West.'"

"Don't get chocolate smudges on the picture!" Joe snatched the photo from Sara's hand and laid it gently on the table. "I am so going to make the guys at work jealous with this baby. I mean, look how sweet she is in that outfit."

"Want some of my soda? You didn't get any." Sara passed over her Coke can.

"I shouldn't, but okay, thanks." Joe took a long pull on the straw. "You know, I don't understand what happened to you. You're not the shy type."

"That's true. But when I stood there in front of Adam West and looked into his deep blue eyes, I just froze." Sara started to open the Butterfinger bar. "You know, this happened to me one other time. I was at Bingo with Gertie a few years back, and I needed one number to be called so that I could have a winner. Sure enough, the guy calls my number, and all I can do is stare at my card. My mother, thank God, looked over and saw that I had the winning number. She told me to say 'Bingo', but I couldn't. She was furious. She yelled 'Bingo' for me, and I won $175. I should have given the money to Gertie, but you know she never would have taken it. Anyway, she wouldn't speak to me for the rest of the night."

"Maybe you have a fear of success."

She had to snort. "I don't think so. Where did you get that crock, from a magazine article? Okay, I become a statue when something seems so incredible that I can't believe it's happening to me. I guess I need a push when I'm in that type of situation."

"Sorry I wasn't there when you met Adam. I wouldn't have taken off if I'd known you would screw up your one big chance so badly."

"Gee, thanks."

"Do you want to try again?" Joe asked. "I mean, we could go back there and you could do it right this time. I'd be there to give you that big push and loan you the extra fifty dollars."

"Actually, I'm thinking about doing that."

"So let's leave these chocolate bars for less fortunate geeks and hightail it over to the autograph area."

"I'm with you, Geek Man." Sara picked up her purse and photograph. The two walked quickly through the throngs, excusing themselves as they bumped into creatures with wings and without proper skin coverage. "I don't think I could ever get used to this."

"What, the fairies? They're kind of neat in a plump, glittery sort of way." Joe grinned at a particularly fetching red-haired fairy with fuchsia wings, her ample bosom dusted with sparking crystals.

"Yeah, the fairies are okay," Sara said, "but put them with the dragon hybrids, the fuzzy neon anime bears and the stormtroopers? You have a freak fest."

"Let's not forget, you are a Bat-fan," Joe said. "Mundanes would lump you in with the others."

"Mundanes?"

"Non-fans. Nowadays the kids call them 'muggles.'"

"But Bat-fandom seems so innocent. I mean, I'm not dressed up as some succubus or zombie girl. I'm just crazy old me of the last generation." Sara rolled her eyes. "Crazy Sara who is willing to pay another fifty dollars to wait another hour in line to say 'thank you,' once more with feeling."

They stopped abruptly. They were at Adam West's table, but there was no Adam West. There was no line of fans; there was only the beefy security staffer, looming like one of the hounds of hell. Sara could almost smell the sulfur breath.

Sara cried, "He's gone!"

"Yes," said Hell Hound. "Mr. West has gone back to his hotel."

"When will he be back?" Sara asked, worry threading her voice. She envisioned an hour wait just for Adam to return from his lunch break, then another hour when the other fans raced back to their places in line. "Where did all the fans go?"

"He won't be back," Hell Hound announced. "As for the other fans—"

Joe joined Sara with the inquisition. "Why did he leave? This doesn't make any sense."

The hound sighed at their ignorance. "He left because he had a prior commitment. If you'd read the sign, you'd'a known."

"What sign?" Sara looked at the back curtain, at the drape around the table, and did a 360-sweep of the area. There was no sign.

Hell Hound stepped to her left, and there, taped to the white tablecloth of Adam's table was a small white piece of paper that read, 'Mr. West will be signing autographs between 10:00 and 12:00 only today.'"

Sara hadn't seen that sign when she had passed the table previously. She didn't remember anything being in that spot. As a teacher, she had a reflexive habit of reading any and all signs. She would have read that one, had it been there. Perhaps some staffer's butt had blocked her view of that sign before, just as Hell Hound's had now.

"But what about all the other people in line?" asked Sara. "There were hundreds of them! What happened to them?"

"How should I know what happened to them? Maybe they left to find a good therapist."

Seeing from Sara's glare that she was probably out of line, Hell Hound took a breath of the fresh air they didn't get in her accustomed domain. When she spoke again, her tone was almost civil. "Mr. West signed for everyone in line until noon. Those who were still in line after 12:00 were out of luck. Hey, if you read the sign, you knew the risk."

Sara turned to Joe. " I guess I should be glad I have this." She waved her black and white photo in the air briefly. For just a moment, tears threatened to come to her eyes.

Knock it off, Goode! Her inner voice admonished her. *You're a grown woman! Hell, you're a middle-aged woman!*

She turned her back on Hell Hound, counting on Joe to follow, and retreated from this convention center Waterloo.

"God," said Joe, catching up to her, "there must have been a geek mutiny. I don't want to think about what you would have done if you'd still been in line when Adam left." He shivered in horror.

"I would have had to spay the Hell Hound," said Sara.

"Who? Oh, you mean that staffer lady?" asked Joe.

"'Lady' is a stretch. But yeah." She sighed. "And, no, I wouldn't have touched her. I'd have broken from the line and run up to Mr. West's table, sobbing and begging him to give me the one last autograph. I'd have told him that I've admired him forever."

"He'd have remembered you then—the lunatic who got carted from the con in cuffs."

"Nice alliteration."

"Anyway, it's not fair to say you've admired him *forever.* You forgot about him for decades."

"But I remember him now!"

Joe looked at her primly. "Doesn't count. Has to be consecutive years. It's in the Holy Fan Handbook of Antioch."

"Is there really—?"

"My *God* you are gullible!"

Sara was more sure than ever that he and Jen would be the perfect couple.

"Then the heck with your rules," said Sara. "I'd tell him that I was dying and that I only had one month to live."

"Bad plan. He's a professional; he'd smell your bad acting a mile away." Joe reached over and brushed a fairy's errant feather from Sara's shoulder.

"I'd cry."

Joe scowled cynically. "Crocodile tears are a woman's last resort."

"I used it on Johnny when we were in high school. It worked. Sometimes." She surreptitiously wiped her eyes with the back of her hand.

"And yet, it didn't stop him from going all the way with Denise."

"Unfortunately, true," Sara admitted.

"Let's blow this joint. I need some fresh air. The stink of some of these fanboys is enough to make me cry for Mama's lavender air freshener."

Exiting the convention center, they blinked hard in the Toronto sunshine. Across the street was a cement park with fountains and anchored metal chairs and tables. Joe and Sara sat down and turned their chairs to face the traffic on the main boulevard.

"Wouldn't you rather go down to the waterfront?" Sara asked Joe. The smell of exhaust from the traffic coupled with the afternoon heat put a chokehold on her breathing. "I don't know about you, but this isn't my idea of fresh air."

"Heck, no, and miss the sights?" Joe's voice sounded reverential.

Sara turned her head to follow his gaze, and almost fell off her chair. Walking, or rather, strutting, down the sidewalk in front of them was a twenty-something brunette beauty in five-inch heels and with her breasts barely restrained by the fabric of her blouse. At that same moment, Sara noticed a black limousine pull up the street and then stop just a short distance in front of the stunning girl. The girl walked on by the limousine without a break in her stride. Within a few seconds of her passing, the limo pulled back out into the traffic and headed towards a hotel complex.

Joe and Sara looked at each other. He ventured, "You don't think?"

"I don't think what?" Sara turned back to watch a fanboy fall off the curb as he spotted the buxom beauty.

"That your Batman, Adam West, was in the limo."

"Oh, surely not."

"Once a ladies man, always a ladies' man." Joe nodded to himself. "I think I've just had one of my questions answered."

"What question?" Sara asked.

"Remember when we watched *Return to the Batcave* at your house, we wondered if the things in the movie were based on real life?" Joe asked.

"Yes."

"Well, after all I've seen and heard, I'm putting two and two together and it's all adding up. Adam West was a player."

Sara had had enough. This was her childhood hero that Joe was maligning.

"Listen, drama queen," she said. "You saw a limo pull up beside an attractive girl, and from that you assume that Mr. West was a playboy. You're reaching pretty far."

"And, you, my dear, are a hopeless Bat-geek. I should leave you here in Toronto with that fan boy you met in the autograph line." Joe straightened the collar of his shirt in his perfectly prissy way. "It would be a love match made in Bat-heaven."

"You wouldn't do that to me," Sara said to Joe. "You're way too nice."

Joe winked. "You're right; I am nice. But the reason I wouldn't leave you here has everything to do with answering to Johnny when I get back. Now let's put that toy car of yours on the road. We have miles to go, and the way you drive, it will be a long while before we sleep."

CHAPTER ELEVEN

The doorbell rang, and Sara froze—right where she was standing in the middle of her living room. It was Monday afternoon. She wasn't expecting company, and she had stripped off her work clothes except for her bra and panties. She'd intended a quick change before taking Dog for a late afternoon walk. Pittsburgh was in full spring bloom, and she hoped to gather a daffodil or two for her kitchen table from a neighbor's garden. She went to grab a quick glass of ice water in the kitchen before putting on sneakers, T-shirt and jeans. Now she was caught, literally, with her pants down.

Dog's incessant barking forced her to attend the unexpected visitor.

The doorbell rang again, followed by staccato knocking on Sara's front door.

"Sara, are you there? It's Nicole. Open up."

Nicole sounded so frantic that Sara yanked the door open, bra and panties in full view of anyone on the street, to find her sister with pain etched on her face. "Nicky! What's going on?"

Nicole grimaced, and then held out a well-toned, high-heeled leg towards Sara.

"New Ferragamos. They…are…*killing*…me!"

Sara looked down at the strappy shoes with the three-inch heels. Nicky's ankles were clearly swelling over the sides of the finely made, impossibly narrow shoes. It was a true emergency, at least in

Nicky's eyes—or rather, on Nicky's feet—and so she knew the walk would have to wait. Dog seemed perfectly content weaving in and around Nicky's legs.

"Kick off those nasty shoes and grab a seat," Sara ordered as she closed the door with a reluctant sigh. "Can I get you anything to drink?"

Eyeing the glass in Sara's hand, Nicky said, "An ice water with lemon would be divine." She looked down at Dog. "Hello, Dog." Dog wagged his tail ecstatically at this new distraction.

"Coming right up." As Sara walked away she heard one plop, then a second one, as Nicole rid herself of her shoes by kicking them across the room. Dog would certainly enjoy those designer shoes as his new play toys. She grabbed her pink chenille robe, fixed a second glass of water, this time with lemon.

"Ah, sweet relief." Nicole had buried her sore pedicured toes into the beige pile carpeting. "This just might be better than sex."

Nicole accepted the sweating glass and drank deeply.

"Don't let Carlos hear you say that, Nicky. Apparently Latin lovers take their sexual prowess very seriously." Sara leaned in towards her sister. "Do they, Nick? Hmm? Inquiring minds want to know."

"Never you mind," Nicole gave a self-satisfied smile that left Sara with the feeling that her sister generally got her share of hot tamales in her chili. "So, how was Toronto? You got back Saturday, right?"

"The car ride was a nightmare—six hours with Joe Norris—each way. You do the math." She collapsed onto her couch, across from the easy chair that held Nicky, her sore feet dangling over the side of the armrest.

"And?" Nicky probed. "Did you get to talk to the great Adam West?"

"Mmmm…no. Not really." Sara drank down the rest of her water, then quietly burped. "The mission was a failure."

Nicole took another sip of her water after delicately squeezing the lemon slice for a few more drops of juice. "They didn't let you get near Adam West, did they? I knew it. Actors have all sorts of entourages these days."

Sara whimpered a little. "Oh, Nick. If only I could blame it on something like that. Actually, I got within a foot of the guy, and I froze like a lily-livered, yellow-bellied coward."

Nicole's eyes widened to the size of saucers. "Get out!"

"I'm telling you the truth, Nicky. Adam looked right at me, and all I could say was 'thank you' in this weird, squeaky voice. It was like I was twelve years old, and I was meeting Davy Jones from the Monkees or something. I think I blushed, too. I'm surprised I didn't grow a zit on the end of my nose on the spot."

Sara shuddered in humiliation and disgust. "He was right *there*. I mean, I could have reached over and touched his big gorgeous Adam West hand, he was that close." The memory of her moment of shame caused a shiver to run through her. "I had a speech all rehearsed, about how I loved his Batman and how it affected me. Blah, blah, blah."

For some reason, probably her unbalanced emotional state, Sara started to laugh. "I am such a loser." The laughter began to take control of her, and she leaned over her armchair, shaking with mirth. "Loser with a capital L." Sara made an L sign against her forehead.

Nicole stared in disbelief. "Good grief, Sara, get a grip on yourself. Here, take a sip of my water." Nicky extended the glass towards her sister. Somewhere along the line, Sara had lost her glass in the cushions of the sofa.

It was all Sara could do to keep her fingers around the sweaty glass, but she managed to drink the lemony cold water between gasps of laughter. Sara breathed in deeply to quiet down and gain some control.

"Phew. That felt good—to laugh, I mean. I am so wired from an entire day with Joe, then my big freeze with Adam West. Yesterday was lesson planning, and today was a full day of school—munchkins with spring fever. It's more than one woman should have to bear." Sara took another sip of water and handed the glass back to Nicole. "Thanks. Oh, and another thanks for looking after Goldie. She's none the worse for the wear."

"No problem. That's what sisters are for." Nicky smiled and gave Sara a soft punch in the arm. "So, are you going to try and see Adam West at another event?"

"Oh, sure. I'd be like, 'Hello, Mr. West, I'll be your stalker for this year. Don't mind me, but I'll be shadowing your every move. I'll be at science fiction conventions from coast to coast, standing in line with the fanboys and clutching my fifty dollars so that I can finally, finally, say thanks for the memories, Batman.'"

"You would do it again, wouldn't you?"

"In a heartbeat."

Sara began to wonder if a life of geekdom was in her future. Would that mean wearing T-shirts emblazoned with, "Beam me up, Scotty" or "Beware of dragons, for you are crunchy and taste good with ketchup?" Living on chocolate bars from convention center concession stands nationwide? Getting varicose veins from standing for hours in autograph lines?

"I fear for you." said Nicky, as though, in addition to hearing Sara's confession, she could read her thoughts right now.

"Yeah, well, the line forms on the left, and I'm the first person in it." Sara shook her head. "This thing with Adam has me stumped."

"Take two aspirin, and maybe you'll feel better in the morning," Nicky said.

Sara gave a wry twist of her lips. "If only…"

"You know, don't you, that this is all just a manifestation of your repressed longing for love and affection?" Nicky was writing Carlos' name in the condensation of her glass.

Yeah, thought Sara, *and I'm the one with the problem.*

"Where did you hear that bit of wisdom, on an Oprah rerun?"

"No, Dr. Phil."

Nicky was a talk show addict. Sara knew that she kept an iPad hidden in her desk drawer at work. The bud in her ear was more likely to be feeding her pop psychology from a celebrity host than any dictation her boss had given her.

"If I had a nickel for every person who has given me some sort of packaged advice, I would have…around twenty cents." Sara said. "But, yeah, you're right. It probably is a manifestation of some psychological mumbo-jumbo. So what should I do, go and get my head examined?"

Nicky tapped her front teeth thoughtfully with a long polished fingernail. "Let's get you hooked up with a prime specimen of the male species. Then you won't need to go to any more nerdy conventions."

"Nicole, I've taken a good look around Pittsburgh, and there's a dearth of what you call 'prime specimens.'" As a normal, red-blooded female, Sara was inclined to check out the many men around town, but besides some hot Steelers football players and the occasional Canadian transplant on the Penguins hockey team, she felt there wasn't much she could see getting worked up about.

Nicole nodded her head up and down in slow agreement. "I take it that Johnny is not on your romance radar?"

"Oh, he's on my radar, all right. But I need to keep him as a friend."

"Okay. Let's go on this assumption that Johnny's not the guy for you, despite the fact that everyone knows that you two would be perfect together." Nicole paused and raised her eyebrows.

"Moving right along..."

"Yes, well..." Nicole reached into her purse and rattled around inside it until she pulled out a small leather-bound notebook. "Let's see who is available."

"You have a little black book? I thought only guys in the seventies had those."

Nicky began flipping through her tiny book, page by page. "We're liberated, Sis! Join the revolution."

"Then why do you still wear high heels? You know, the ones that are lying on my floor because they were killing you? We fought hard for the right to wear flat shoes and pants to work, Nicky."

Nicky pouted. She wasn't ready to admit that she wore those shoes to attract men. "They make my calves look damn good. It's a personal choice."

"Mm-hmm," said Sara.

"Oh, look, Jeremy Walsh!" Nicky pointed dramatically to an entry in her little black book. "He's a diamond in the rough. Perfect."

"If he's so perfect, then why aren't you dating him?"

"I did, for a while. Then Carlos moved to town. I broke poor Jeremy's heart, but you're just the girl to make him forget all about me." Nicky's eyes shone brightly as she contemplated her matchmaking.

"Do you really think a guy would date the sister of the woman who dumped him?"

"He's a man, Sara. They don't think like we do. It wouldn't occur to Jeremy that the situation might be a bit...indelicate."

"Great. You make this guy seem so sensitive. He's sure to be my dream boat."

"Honey, it's not just him," Nicky said. "They're all simple creatures. They need us women to prod them into making the right moves. And Jeremy does have the sweetest dimples."

"I am a sucker for dimples." Sara admitted. She looked out her living room window at the golden sunlight of late afternoon. She considered the idea of meeting a new man, sharing her stories, going out on a real date, experiencing a sweet goodnight kiss, waiting by the phone for a call that would never come, running into the guy with his arm around another girl at some nightclub down in the Strip District, waking up almost-too-late for work due to a crashing hangover after a pity party and at least one whole bottle of wine...

"No, Nicky. I can't do it. I don't care if his dimples have dimples. I won't go on a blind date and that's my final answer." Sara got up and loped off to the kitchen for something to snack on, something to quiet the anxiety running through her body. *So much for a nice, peaceful walk through the neighborhood with Dog.* She grabbed a bag of M&M's from the cupboard, ripped it open and proceeded to pop chocolate morsels into her mouth at lightning speed. She was dimly aware that chocolate was a running theme in her life lately, but she quickly fed those anxious thoughts another dozen M&Ms. Dog, having the acute hearing of any household pet, came running at the sound of the crinkling snack bag.

"Oh, no you don't," Sara said. "I don't want you getting sick and ruining your chances to be adopted by some family." Dog gave a sharp bark, which Sara ignored.

Nicky, following Dog into the kitchen, asked, "What the hell are you doing?" Sara felt that, for someone with swollen feet, Nicky sure moved quickly.

Sara garbled her initial words since her mouth was filled with chocolate. "Ahem. I was, um, having a little snack."

Nicky put her hands on her hips and shook her head sorrowfully. "What are we going to do with you, Sara?"

Sara made a pathetic smile. "Love me?"

"Well, for starters, I'm taking this bag of sugar away from you and putting it in a place where you won't find it."

Sara reluctantly handed over the candy bag and then raised her head defiantly. "You can have my candy, but you can never make me go on a blind date. Right, Dog?"

Dog gave another bark then trotted over to the cabinet with the dog treats. Sara grabbed a few milk bones for Dog. His tail wagging furiously, he triumphantly ran from the kitchen with the treats in his mouth.

"Okay, okay," Nicky tried to appease Sara in a soft soothing tone. It did aggravate Sara when Nicky tossed a handful of the M&M's into her own mouth before walking back to the living room to stow the candy bag in her purse. Sara took some pleasure in the fact that Nicky winced from the pain in her feet with every step.

Nicky sauntered back to the kitchen, acting as if she hadn't stolen Sara's last hope for achieving chocolate bliss. "We're going to have to come up with another idea. Let me think."

Nicky pulled out a kitchen chair at the retro chrome table and sat down. Sara opened a few more cabinets, trying to find a treat that would satisfy the deep craving that the chocolate had awakened in her. She was pretty sure that pretzels weren't going to do the trick.

"Oh, I know!" Nicky's exclamation startled her, and Sara upended a box of buttery crackers.

"Sara, put the food away and come sit down with me. I think I have the answer to your difficulty in meeting men." Sara pushed the broken crackers into the sink and washed them down the disposal. Rubbing cracker crumbs off her hands, she turned and gave her sister the evil eye.

"I do not, for your information, have difficulty meeting men," Sara said. "I just can't seem to find one that I want to keep around."

Nicky tapped her fingertips on the table. "The way I see it, the whole problem comes down to this. You are obsessed with thanking Adam West for his Batman performance, but you are probably focusing on him because you'd rather do that than face up to your wrecked marriage. In addition, you are exceedingly picky about who you date, and that limits your choices. I think you need to go out with a guy, maybe a lot of guys, to see that you can be having a lot more fun in your life."

"Everyone thinks they can fix me," Sara commented. "Joe thinks I'm hung up because of my age, and you think I need to date lots of men to put the disaster of my marriage behind me."

"Truthfully, I think you're too scared to get back up on that horse."

"Gee, thanks. I think." Sara really was getting exasperated. No one had the right to criticize the way she was living her life. She was doing the best she could, and truthfully, she felt that she was doing a pretty good job of being a success. Sara had a terrific teaching job, a bunch of wonderful friends, and her eccentric family to keep her happy.

"We're going to have a party," Nicole announced.

"Huh?" Sara asked. She couldn't see how Nicky's conversation about dating had led to the idea of a party.

"We'll have a party right here, in your house. How about the Saturday after next? Everyone—friends and family—will invite an acceptable guy for you to meet, here in the safety of your own home."

Nicky looked so proud of herself, Sara hated to have to burst her bubble. "How are you going to get all my friends, including you, and I assume Mom as well, to agree on who is the most acceptable guy for me to meet?"

"That's the beauty of this plan, Sara. There won't be just one guy. Everyone will invite their own idea of the perfect guy for you. That way there will be a room full of eligible guys for you to meet and the odds of your finding a match will be greater."

"Ooh," Sara said. "I have a bad feeling about this."

"We'll have it catered so that you won't have to worry about the details on party night. All you'll have to do is focus on looking sexy and making a good impression on all the guys that'll be here."

"That's all? Look sexy and attract hordes of men? Piece of cake." Sara started chuckling at the thought of sitting on the couch surrounded by suitors, a modern-day Scarlett O'Hara at the Wilkes plantation. "Now Nicole, won't it look strange to have a room full of eligible guys lining up to meet me while the rest of you stand around watching? I mean, come on! Any normal guy would hightail it out of here as fast as a meatball slips off a hoagie roll."

Nicky held up her hands to stop Sara's ranting. "Yes, we'll all invite any eligible guy we know, but we will also invite other people to fill the room and make the actual purpose of the evening less obvious. It'll be a party, except there will be the added agenda of hoping you make a connection with one of the guys."

"I don't want any pressure from any of you. If something comes out of the party, then fine. But I don't want you all breathing down my neck. Got it?" Sara said firmly.

"You won't regret it, Sara." Nicole stood up and gave her sister a huge hug. "Oh, I can't wait. This is going to be so much fun. I've got to get home and make some calls."

"Don't forget your shoes," Sara reminded her. "Unless you want to leave them for Dog to chew."

Nicole looked down at her red, swollen feet. "Um, Sara, could I borrow a pair of your slippers? There's no way I'm going to get my feet back into those heels."

"So sayeth my liberated sister." Sara went to her bedroom closet and selected her bright yellow quacking duck ones—the last that hadn't been chewed up by Dog.

Karma's a bitch, Nicky.

Nicky called after Sara. "Hey, I love high heels, and you have thing for Batman. So what's the difference?"

Sara enjoyed the idea that Nicky was going to be pegged as the crazy lady in duckie slippers. "Fine. We're both nuts. Only, if I get my chance to thank Adam West properly, my problem is over. You, however, will continue to live a life of high-heeled pain."

Sara grabbed hold of the slippers that were hidden under her bed. They had been gnawed on only slightly. She smugly held them in front of her as she returned to the living room.

Nicky moaned, "Not the duckie slippers!"

"Oh, yes, dear sister." Sara smiled wickedly. "This is the price you must pay for wanting to hold a party right here in my quiet, peaceful home."

"Fine." Nicky grabbed the slippers from Sara. "I'll wear the damn things. But you better start thinking about how you're going to handle this party. Oh, and Sara, I'd keep that Batman obsession under wraps during the party. It is a little weird, you know."

"Says the woman who's got Donald and Daisy on her feet."

CHAPTER TWELVE

"What's up, Sara?" asked Charlotte, licking chocolate pudding off her spoon. Char had been watching Sara intently. "You're way too quiet. I don't think you've said a word since you sat down."

"Hmm," Sara replied absently. She picked at her salad, pushing aside the dark lettuce leaves for the succulent lighter leaves below.

Char looked to Jen, who shrugged her shoulders. They both turned to stare at Sara.

Sara audibly exhaled and put her fork down on the table. As she raised her eyes, she met the stares of her friends. "What? What did I do?"

"Spill the beans, Goode," ordered Jen.

"I'm sorry. I have a lot going on right now," Sara said. "I'm stressed about the end of the school year, what with final grading and packing up the whole classroom. I still don't understand why returning teachers have to pack up their stuff every summer."

"Two reasons." Jen had seen it all and wasn't surprised at anything after five years in the main office. "The cleaning staff has to be able to fumigate and disinfect every nook and cranny. And then there is always a teacher or two who just decides not to return. They get a position somewhere else, or they throw in the towel completely and go into real estate."

"I suppose," said Sara. "But it still doesn't make the process any easier to take."

"Oh, puh-leeze!" Jen said. "You get to have two entire months off. I, on the other hand, will be here, chained to my desk." Jen took a fierce stab at a cherry tomato on her plate, which sent the tomato flying across the table and on to the floor.

"We're sorry, Jen!" Charlotte leaned over and gave Jen a full-body hug.

Jen pulled away. "For Pete's sake, you didn't do anything, Char. I'm just feeling sorry for myself, same as Sara."

"Don't follow my lead!" laughed Sara, "you'll get nowhere fast."

Charlotte frowned slightly, then said, "You girls need to lighten up. Summer is here, and I'm thrilled to pieces." She started singing, "*Summer lovin', had me a blast…*"

"Oh, so you know *that* classic song, but when I brought up a song by the Monkees, it was like you were born yesterday," Sara said.

"I know lots of musical scores. I am in the Arts, you know." Char flipped back her blonde hair.

Jen and Sara silently nodded their heads, avoiding eye contact with each other so that they wouldn't start giggling.

"I'm anxiously waiting to hear that Dog has a new owner, Char. What's up with that?"

"Yeah, well. It's not as easy as I thought it would be. But don't worry, Sara. I'm sure someone will turn up soon." Char became suddenly interested in her pudding cup.

Sara sighed and turned to Jen. "What's new with the computer caper? Have you and Joe made any progress finding the perp?" Sara asked.

"Funny you should ask. Joe's in the office right now. I asked him to join us for lunch, but he said he was close to solving the crime. Personally, I think he was too intimidated to be in a room where he's outnumbered by women."

"Joe's a big fan of women," said Sara, "but he doesn't feel comfortable being in large groups of females without some buddies to hang with. It's too bad, because he should be taking advantage of this time to get to know you better. He must really be on to something."

Jen blushed, but remained silent.

"I do have some news to share," Sara said. "But I'm not particularly happy with it."

The girls went on high alert. "Oh?" Charlotte asked.

"I don't know if Nicky's called you yet, but she wants to have a party for the sole purpose of having me meet some new guys. I guess she's hoping that something will click and there will be sparks between me and...*someone*. I'm not crazy about the idea. I mean, who wants a group of strangers all over their house? It feels tawdry."

"It's not tawdry; I think it's brilliant!" Jen swung her iced tea glass towards Sara as if making a toast. "Nicole is just trying to get you acclimated to Pittsburgh and wants you to have someone to explore the area with."

Sara guffawed. "Acclimated, Jen? I've been here for a year already. I've been hanging out with you gals after work and on the weekends. We've hit the stores, seen shows at the Benedum and eaten in every restaurant between here and Lake Erie. I consider myself acclimated."

"Come on, Sara," Charlotte said, intervening. "You know what she means. It's time to find a nice guy to see the sights with."

"Someone who will treat you special and give you all the attention you deserve," Jen added.

Sara closed her eyes and took a deep breath. "You know, girls, I'm doing just fine. I'm starting to get a little peeved because everyone I know is poking their nose into my love life. Even Joe has been nagging me about it. So for the record, I'm not in the market for a man. I know you two are at the beginning of your relationships with some great guys and want to spread your joy all around. But I'm quite sure that I don't need a man to complete me, or to find happiness in my life. Okay?"

"Does this mean that there won't be a party?" Char asked meekly.

Sara thought for a few moments then shook her head. "No. There will be a party, I promised Nicole in a moment of weakness, so I have to go through with it. But I'll be at the party on my own terms, got it?"

Jen and Charlotte both agreed to Sara's terms with nodding heads and full smiles. Sara knew what those smiles meant: Jen was secretly compiling a list of men to invite; Charlotte was envisioning a sexy outfit to impress Mitchell on the night of the party.

Sara had begun to munch on a chocolate chip cookie when she spied Joe entering the lunch room. "Well, what do you know? Joe isn't afraid of women, after all."

The girls turned to greet Joe as he reached the table. "Hi, ladies. Do I still have time to join you before the bell rings?" He dumped a paper bag on the table and removed a sandwich and an orange.

"Pull up a chair, stranger," Sara said. "Long time no see since our lightning raid on Toronto."

Joe gave a half-hearted snarl, then went to grab an empty chair across the room. He returned saying, "You're not going to believe what I just found out about the hacker."

"Shh," Sara said *sotto voce*. "There are a lot of elephant ears around here."

"Not to mention other elephant parts. Have you seen what Cissie Bolton has packed in her lunch? Ding-Dongs. And she calls herself an educator." Joe grimaced at the idea of so many empty calories.

"Come on, Joe," Jen said. "Focus and tell us about the school hacker. It's one of the Nelson brothers, isn't it? Those kids are always finding trouble."

Joe took a bite of his sandwich, and in between chews, he answered, "You have to swear on a stack of dictionaries, or whatever it is you school people worship, that the name I give you won't go further than this table."

"You have our word," whispered Charlotte.

Joe nodded. "Okay, well, after some fancy footwork I found out that the hacker is…Mr. Johnson's grandson!"

The girls were shocked. "Nooo!" exclaimed Jen. "That can't be right. Please tell me you're joking."

"Can't do that. Danny Johnson is our man, er, boy." Joe placed a hand on Jen's arm. "I'm sorry, Jen. I know Principal Johnson is your boss, and things are going to get uncomfortable when he finds out it's his grandson."

"Hoo-boy. You have no idea how Mr. Johnson is going to take this. He wanted to make an example of the student who was named as the hacker. Now that the hacker is his grandson, I can't imagine what he'll do." Jen nervously folded her napkin into smaller and smaller squares.

"He'll still have to let everyone know, including the school staff, the district and the PTA. You can't hush up something like this, especially since he made such a big issue of it when it was first discovered. If he had presented a calmer front, then he wouldn't be in this awkward position right now," Joe said.

"I don't feel good," said Jen. She began gathering her sandwich wrappers and napkins in a pile on the table. "I can't believe this is happening."

Joe wolfed down the remainder of his sandwich then shoved his orange back into his bag. "Listen, Jen. I'll go with you and we can tell Mr. Johnson together."

Jen clutched her stomach and moaned. "Seriously, I'm going to be sick."

Sara grabbed Jen's hand. "You'll be fine; you can do this. Char and I will be here if you need us."

Jen stood up slowly. "This sucks. Why couldn't it have been one of the juvenile delinquents at this place? Danny has never acted up; he's one of the good kids, or so I thought."

"Sometimes good people make bad mistakes," said Sara. "The kid is going to have to own up to this one and suffer the consequences. Maybe he'll learn a lesson along the way."

"He could be expelled," Jen said. "That's one hell of a lesson." She stood up and threw away her trash. Joe cupped her elbow in his hand and guided her through the crowded lunch room.

"Look at the love birds!" crowed Cissie Bolton. "Aren't they sweet together?" The other Queen Bee teachers tittered at the comment.

Sara frowned, and said, "If they only knew what those two are facing."

Char wrinkled her nose in distaste. "Oh, they'll hear all about it before the end of the day. The school grapevine is alive and well at May View Elementary."

"Here's hoping that the stress of this situation doesn't cause Joe and Jen to go their separate ways," Sara said. "Things seem to be going so well."

"I'm sure they'll be okay. But Mr. Johnson? He may be packing up his office at the same time that we're emptying out our classrooms."

Sara stood up. "Sorry to ditch you early, Char, but I have some things to do in the classroom before the kids get back from recess."

Char waved her hand at Sara. "Sure, sure. I'm almost done here, too. See ya."

Sara walked briskly back to her classroom, sat down at her desk, opened her laptop, started a new document in Word... And began to write another letter to Adam West.

There were so many reasons—she wanted to tell him how exciting it had been to see him in Toronto; how dismayed she'd been when she couldn't find the words to speak to him. She also wanted to let him know how disappointing it was that he had left the convention early. After all, there were fans, namely her, waiting to spend for precious one-on-one time with him. Most of all, she wanted—needed—to make him understand her quest to meet him.

Sara knew her whirlwind trip with Joe was about more than saying a heartfelt "thank you" to Mr. West, though that was the rationale she had used. It was about understanding this... *obsession* with the actor who had played Batman decades ago. And that was the same reason she was writing the second letter—not to tell Adam West anything, but to make *herself* understand, well, herself.

> *Dear Mr. West,*
>
> *I met you at the Toronto Science Fiction Convention last weekend. I'm so grateful for the opportunity to meet you in person. I'm afraid I made a bit of a fool of myself. I got completely tongue-tied when it came time to actually talk to you. You graciously signed your autograph on my photo, but I didn't get to actually say anything. I actually came back to pay for another photo so I could talk to you again.*

I was disappointed to learn that you had left the convention early. I had hoped to get a second chance to express my gratitude and admiration for your work as Batman. You had a big impact on my life.

I wrote a long letter to you a month ago, telling you of my delight at rediscovering you after several decades. Although I am still the biggest Adam West fan around, and your portrayal of Batman will always be my favorite, I understand that my intense focus on you was prompted by emotional upheaval in my own life. Instead of facing my own issues, I decided to escape into Gotham City.

I think I'm ready to step forward and make a change. To let down my guard and allow others into my life...I think.

Of course, by others I mean men, and that would put me at risk for more pain, like I experienced in my divorce, like I experienced when my first love broke my heart. Maybe I should stay solitary like Batman, devoting myself to my teaching and staying far from trouble.

You see, I'm not sure what I should do. But Batman? Batman would always know what to do. I guess that's why I was trying so hard to make him — to make you — part of my life.

Anyway, those are the thoughts of a fifty-year fan. Those thoughts, and...Thank you, Mr. West. Thank you for everything.

— Sara Goode

Sara closed her laptop with a satisfied smile. She would mail the letter on the way home from work. He wouldn't respond to this letter, either, but it felt good to put it down on paper. At least she was facing her mid-life crisis head-on.

CHAPTER THIRTEEN

Sara checked the rearview mirror of her Mini Cooper. Then she checked it again. Sure enough, she was being followed home from work. The car behind her was keeping its distance, but it was also imitating Sara's every move. Left on Sunrise. Right on Irishtown Road. Sara picked up speed on Connor Road, hoping to lose the other car by speeding through an "orange" light. But of course, all the lights remained green. Sara couldn't remember a time when all the lights had stayed green—an oddity worthy of sharing with the gals at the hair salon. Of course, if she didn't lose this driver and he turned out to be a serial killer, she would never visit any salon again.

Her pursuer's car was bright red, a new model sedan, with trim suggesting a special edition package. The front windows were slightly tinted, and, with the addition of the late afternoon sun glinting off the glass, Sara had a hard time making out the features of the driver's face.

In a move designed to save her life, Sara swerved quickly into the parking lot of the gas station at the corner of Connor and Jefferson roads. She popped open the door latches before she had even put the car in park. She leapt from the driver's seat, clutching her handbag, and raced into the mini-mart. As she tugged at the door, she imagined the driver from the red car inches behind her, weapon in hand. She could almost feel his breath on her neck. Inside the store, she dashed behind a Valvoline display. She was breathing so fast, she thought her heart would burst out of her chest.

"Sara?" A familiar voice from the cold drink case made her turn her head.

"Johnny?" Sara couldn't believe it. The one time she needed a hero, there was Johnny. She could have kissed him right then and there. "Johnny! Oh, God, Johnny! I need your help!" She grabbed his arm like a drowning woman would a lifesaver. "There's a guy that's following me in a red sports car! I don't know what's going on. I'm really scared."

"Ow! Geez, Sara! Let go. Everything's fine." Johnny pulled from her grasp and took a step away from her.

"Easy for you to say. You're not the one who's being followed!"

"But I am the one who's following you." Johnny put his hands on Sara's shoulders and looked into her eyes. "But I didn't mean to scare you, Sara. I swear."

"Since when do you have a red car?"

"I've had it since Saturday. I'm sorry. I forgot that you were away last weekend and hadn't seen my new wheels," said Johnny.

Sara peered around the display of motor oil and looked around. No bad guys in sight, just the Pakistani owner, sitting behind the cash register, and a little old guy who was checking out the loose tobacco brands at the front counter. "Hmm," she said.

"Come on, how many crazed lunatics are there with a penchant for chicks in yellow go-carts?"

"It's a Mini Cooper, not a go-cart. Okay, prove it was you—how many red lights did I hit on Connor Road?" asked Sara.

"None. Wasn't that *weird*?"

Sara sighed in relief. "Okay, you're legit." She peered at him closely. "Why were you following me? Couldn't you have called my cell? Instead of scaring me out of my wits?"

"I tried, I swear. But your phone must be on silent."

Sara rummaged for her slim phone. "Well, how about that? It seems it's powered off. Wouldn't hear it ring that way, nope." Sara smiled sheepishly at Johnny. "I keep it off during the school day. You know, school policy."

"How is anyone supposed to reach you in an emergency?"

"The principal feels that if something is urgent enough, we can be reached through the school secretary's phone line."

"Stupid."

"Yeah. What else is new?" Sara started for the door. "Nothing today. Maybe tomorrow," she said apologetically as she passed the owner.

He waved pleasantly, so she didn't feel too guilty about using his store as a hideout. Sara walked towards Johnny's new car, Johnny trailing behind her.

"Wow. Now that I know I won't be taking my last ride in its trunk, this car is a beaut," Sara smirked devilishly at Johnny. "Isn't that what you guys say to each other? It's a beaut, yessiree, a real beaut."

"I'll tell you who's a *real* beaut—"

"Uh, uh, uh. No wolfish come-ons. You need to be a gentleman. You scared me out of my wits, and that's the price."

"For how long?" Johnny asked.

"Oh, how long do you have to be nice to me? Probably forever."

"Never mind," Johnny clicked the remote. Sara opened the door and deeply inhaled the delightful new car smell.

Getting in next to her, Johnny said, "Listen, Sara, there's something I want you to see, but it entails a bit of trust on your part. How about if you drive your car home, and I'll meet you there? I promise not to follow too closely."

"I suppose." Sara shrugged acceptance.

"You'll get to ride in my new car and enjoy that new car smell to your heart's delight." He waggled his eyebrows enticingly.

"Okay, if you promise not to do that thing with your eyebrows again."

"Deal."

Sara once again got into her compact car and headed for home. This time, seeing Johnny's car a respectable distance behind her, she did feel kind of silly for thinking she'd had a maniac on her tail.

Sara parked in her driveway and waited for Johnny. "You can park—" she began.

"No need. Just get in and we'll be off as soon as I put the top down. It's a convertible," he added proudly.

"Kinda figured you wouldn't put the top down otherwise."

Sara looked longingly at her front door. She really just wanted to go inside and relax. "I should feed Dog," she said.

Johnny's expectant face began to fall.

"Alrighty, then. Dog will have to wait for his dinner. Mrs. Blarcom next door has started taking him for a walk at lunchtime so I guess he'll be okay for a little while." She opened the passenger door of his car. "Let's get this show on the road."

"One thing I can always say about you," Johnny said a few moments later as he headed north on Washington Road, toward downtown Pittsburgh. "You're a good sport."

"Oh? And why's that?" Sara asked. She was having a great time with the top down and her hair tangling wildly in the breeze.

"Well, I don't know too many women who'd allow their stalker to take them out for a ride. Especially since I haven't given you a clue about where we're going."

"I guess I thought you were taking me to the new restaurant that you're working for at the Waterfront."

"Nope. Not even close."

"And since you're not really a stalker, I figured that I was in pretty good hands."

"You're right about the good hands part. Oh, what my hands could do if they were given the chance." Johnny leaned towards Sara and incorrigibly ran his fingers under the hem of her skirt.

"Hey, fella!" She slapped his fingers away. "Hands on the wheel and eyes facing ahead at all times."

"Pah. I take back the good sport thing." Johnny sat back with an exaggerated thump, but his smile let Sara know that he loved testing her limits. Besides, he had to concentrate on the traffic now that they were entering the Liberty Tunnel, where lane changers and speeders abounded, despite Pennsylvania's reputation for strict laws and doddering motorists.

"Oh, man. Forgive me, Sara. I forgot we were going through the tunnel." Johnny looked up at the open roof of the car. "We're going to be sucking in some major exhaust."

"Just part of the adventure." She tried to hold her breath for as long as possible then slid her face down inside the front of her shirt. "Besides, I get plenty of fumes in a classroom of kindergarteners. We're talking toxic waste gases. It could make a grown man cry."

Johnny reached over and ruffled Sara's already windswept hair. "You know you're nuts, right?"

"Probably the side effect of the toxic gases."

"Okay. We're out," Johnny announced, unnecessarily. The fresher air and bright sunlight as the car cleared the portal were tells.

Sara straightened to catch the spectacular view of the Pittsburgh skyline. The city wasn't all that big, in comparison to New York or Philadelphia, but it took her breath away every time. The dark glass of the old US Steel building, the outline of PNC Stadium, the glistening rivers and the arc of the bridges made for a visual smorgasbord. Pride in her city filled Sara's chest and made her glad that she had returned to her old hometown.

Johnny exited on Route 19. Sara slid on the seat from the force of the turn on the ramp and couldn't stop herself from bumping into Johnny.

"I knew you wanted me," Johnny said. "Now all you have to do is admit it."

Sara ignored his teasing. "Where are we going?" They were in the lane for the Pittsburgh Convention Center. Johnny pulled past the main doors of the arena and turned into a service driveway. The car engine whined a bit on the steep ramp that took them to a loading dock. The tall doors of the loading bays were closed, and no one was in sight.

"So you wanted to know where we're going, eh? Well, here we are." He turned off the car ignition, got out and came around to open her door.

"You are a gentleman, even if you are a stalker." Sara allowed him to help her out of her seat. She tried to pat down her hair, but it was a lost cause. "I hope we're not attending some fancy event. I am a complete and utter mess."

"You're fine, Sara," Johnny murmured.

Sara peeked at herself in the passenger's side mirror. "But—"

Johnny firmly closed her door and walked toward the loading bays. *Geez,* Sara thought, *I just need a second.*

But, watching Johnny's lovely retreating backside, she decided not to be left alone in the deserted alley. She ran to Johnny, who was busy working a key into the lock of a heavy metal door. One quick twist of the handle, and it opened.

Inside it was darker than night. The door slammed shut behind them, and Sara jumped with a startled, "Oh!"

"Just a sec," Johnny whispered.

Sara heard rustling then squinted as Johnny turned on a bright flashlight. In that darkness, any light would have made a big difference.

"Stand here, and don't move," Johnny said.

Sara gladly froze as he walked away. Within seconds there was a click and then an explosion of light. Nothing could have prepared Sara for the sight that filled her eyes once they adjusted. Nothing.

No more than ten feet away from Sara was the Batmobile.

She blinked in confusion. How could this be? She scanned the rest of the enormous room with its concrete floors and stark brick walls, but it was empty. Except for the Batmobile.

"Okay. What is this? Did you steal the Batmobile?"

Johnny just smiled broadly at the sleek lines of the classic red and black car.

"Seriously, Johnny, what is the Batmobile doing here, in Pittsburgh, in this warehouse or whatever this is?" Sara took a few steps towards the car, and then a few more. She reached out and with the fingers of her right hand she lightly caressed a wing of the car. "Oh," she said. "I'm touching the Batmobile."

Johnny strode to her side, grinning from ear to ear. "Neat, huh?"

Sara was incredulous. "'Neat?' How about unfriggin' believable!" She walked slowly around the car, gazing at the glass-domed windshields, the control panel on the dashboard, the exhaust jets and the red bat symbol on the doors.

"I thought you'd like it. I came to the car show last weekend. Some of my friends were working it, and they just happened to mention knowing the guy who owns this Batmobile. I guess he built it himself. It's exactly like the one they used on TV." Johnny seemed excited to share what he knew about the car. "Anyway, they told me the owner would be storing it here for a few days after the show. His transport truck broke down, and he can't take the car on highways with it only capable of going about 20 miles an hour."

"A car show?" Sara speculated. "Would that be why you suddenly own a new car?"

"When a man has nothing else to spend his money on, it's hard to say no to an opportunity like that one. Anyway, my friends were able to pull a few strings and get me a key. There's a security guy who should be checking in shortly, but don't worry. Everything is cool."

"I guess it pays to know people in high places." Sara stared into the cockpit of the car. She guessed it was a cockpit, she really didn't know about these things. There were two bucket seats, one for Batman and one for his sidekick, Robin, just like in the television show. She standing next to—touching!—a pure and shining symbol of her youth. She was certain that her heart was beating faster than when she met Adam West, if such a thing was possible.

"Want to go for a spin?" Johnny asked.

Sara whipped her head around. "You're kidding, right? Don't play with me, Johnny."

Johnny's laughter bounced off the walls of the cavernous room. "I know better than to tease you with something like this. I wouldn't be able to stand the disappointment in your sweet baby browns. Come on, let's get in." He opened the passenger door for her. "Your Batmobile awaits."

Trembling, Sara slid through the open door of the Batmobile.

Johnny ran to the driver's side and entered in the usual manner. "I'd jump over the door into the seat if I wasn't afraid of hurting myself in awkward places."

Sara had to admit that Johnny looked mighty fine sitting behind the wheel of the Batmobile. He turned the key and revved the engine. "Put your seatbelt on, Batgirl, we're going for a ride!"

Sara clicked on her belt, holding her breath as Johnny pulled the car from its spot and slowly drove the outer perimeter of the stadium-sized room. She could easily see herself fantasizing that she was riding with Batman on their way to solving a major crime caper.

She was surprised that the black leather seats were so comfortable. She nestled back to enjoy the ride.

After two times around the room, Johnny drove the car back to its parking spot. He turned off the ignition, and the room was filled with utter silence.

"My turn," Sara said.

"What do you mean?"

"It's my turn to drive the Batmobile. Let's switch seats, and you can play the sidekick this time."

"Sara, I don't know. I mean, it was kind of understood that I would do the driving..." Johnny looked flustered, an unusual occurrence.

"Now you have a new understanding. I will do the driving." She opened the car door and ran around to the driver's side. With some reluctance, Johnny opened his door and yielded the driver's seat to her.

Sara jumped in and buckled up. "Atomic batteries to power! Turbines to speed!" They were infamous lines recited by Robin, the Boy Wonder, when the Batmobile was starting up to leave the Batcave.

"Wait!" Johnny yelled as fell into his seat and barely closed his door before Sara gunned the accelerator. After an initial lurch, she had the Batmobile under total control and gliding through the room.

"I'm the Queen of the World!" she exclaimed, her voice echoing against the walls of the vast space. She took her hands off the wheel and extended them triumphantly, as Leo DiCaprio had in *Titanic*. Desperately, Johnny grabbed the wheel with one hand had pushed her right arm down with the other to urge her to take control of the vehicle again.

Sara merely laughed. She felt the joy of having an impossible wish come true. She would be able to tell people, "I drove the Batmobile."

"Okay, now nice and easy," Johnny said. "Bring it to a stop by the door where we came in," To his credit, he sounded calm.

Sara was aware that allowing her to drive the Batmobile was a huge risk for him.

But nothing went wrong, and Sara stopped Batmobile close to its original position.

"Holy cannoli! That was amazing." Sara had a grin that stretched for a mile. "I drove the Batmobile. I…drove…the…Batmobile!"

"You sure did. Sorry the trip was so short, but we have to be careful with the exhaust in here, since the room is closed. Usually the cars are only run while the big garage doors are opened."

"Sure. I understand. Johnny, this is the most awesome surprise I've ever had. I'll never be able to thank you enough. I'll try, but I know I won't be able to match this moment you've given me." Sara placed her hand on his arm.

Johnny turned towards her. "Sara." His eyes met hers, and for some reason, no other words were needed. He bent his head towards her, and their lips met softly in a gentle kiss. Sara's heart, which had been slowed almost to normal since parking the Batmobile, now picked up a drumming pace.

"Johnny?" All of her fears and doubts rose within her.

"Shh, Sara. It's okay." Then, Johnny kissed her again, with more intensity and passion than before. Sara eagerly returned his hot kisses, and they were instantly entwined, as much as they could be, in the bucket seats of the Batmobile.

Johnny took Sara's face within both of his hands, his thumbs caressing her cheeks. "I remember you."

Sara wasn't the type to swoon, but her stomach flip-flopped at Johnny's words. "Johnny, what are we doing?" Her thoughts were a tangled mess; nothing seemed to be making sense.

"I'm doing exactly what I've wanted to do since the day you came back to Pennsylvania. Loving you."

At those words, the old fears ripped through Sara like a fault line during an earthquake. Despite her fledgling intentions to open herself to new feelings, she felt a overwhelming urge pull away. She needed to say something to protect herself from the inevitable—the pain that always followed the joy.

A loud voice interrupted. "Hey! You guys okay?"

They turned to see a portly man in a blue security uniform standing in the far shadows of the room.

Johnny cleared his throat and loudly answered, "Fine. We're just fine. We had our ride, and we'll probably be heading home now."

"That's great, 'cause I'm going to have to button down the place soon. Shift change, and I don't want nobody to get in trouble, if yinz know what I mean."

"Oh. Sure." Johnny opened his car door and stood up. "We'll just be another minute then we'll be on our way."

The guard nodded. "Okay. Just be sure to pull that back door tight behind you. And you'll be giving the key back to Sharky, right?"

"First thing tomorrow morning," Johnny assured him.

"Alright then, have a good evening, folks." The guard walked down a hallway and was soon out of sight.

Johnny walked over to Sara's side of the Batmobile. "I guess that's it, Batgirl."

"Yeah," Sara sighed loudly. As she stood, she ran her hand one last time down the smooth, shiny door of the Batmobile. "Thanks, Johnny. This was…" She couldn't finish her sentence.

"Hey, no problem," Johnny and Sara walked out the back door and over to where Johnny's new car was parked.

"Johnny?" Sara asked.

"Yes?" Johnny asked quickly.

"Uh, I have something I have to say. I mean, I want to say." It took all of Sara's courage to speak up.

Johnny smiled, cocking his head quizzically to the side, "Okay."

"Johnny, I'm not sure what happened in there just now. With the kissing. Anyway, I don't want you to get the idea that things between us have changed in some major way. The kissing was great; don't get me wrong. It was really great." Sara grasped his arm gently. "But I'm confused; I need to think things through. I do care about you, I want you to know that. But I need time, to see what's right."

Johnny's shoulders drooped under his sweater. "More time, Sara?"

"Johnny, you got me the Batmobile! That means so much to me, and I don't know if the feelings I had back there are real or just a result of being so excited about living a childhood fantasy."

He took her hand. "But didn't you feel the electricity between us? You were there. You had to have noticed."

Sara shook her head. "Of course I noticed. But Johnny, I'm just not sure. I hope you can forgive me. I hope you can give me more time."

Johnny squeezed her hand. "Well, I guess I'll have to take that for now. Maybe somewhere down the line, Sara?"

Sara stood looking into Johnny's kind and familiar face. "Let's wait and see. Okay?"

Johnny gave a rueful laugh. "Okay. But I'm not going to let this go, Sara. You can count on that." He slipped his hand from hers as they reached his car. "Just be gentle with me. I may be big and muscular, but inside beats a very soft heart."

Sara nodded as she opened the passenger door. She hesitated before slipping into her seat.

"Johnny?" she asked.

"Yes?"

"Were you surprised when I wanted to drive the Batmobile?"

Johnny laughed. "Maybe a little. It didn't even cross my mind that you'd want to do that. But it should have."

"Never underestimate my capacity to surprise you."

"Nope. Never again," he said as he placed both hands on the steering wheel. "You're full of surprises. You're completely... inspired."

"I like that. I'm Sara Goode, driven by inspiration."

"Not to mention, a bit of *chutzpah*," Johnny winked at Sara.

"But, of course!"

Johnny began the drive back to Brighton Park while Sara remained, in spirit, back in the seat of the Batmobile and sharing sweet kisses with Johnny.

CHAPTER FOURTEEN

The lazy days of summer were within Sara's reach. It was Memorial Day weekend, with three glorious days of absolutely nothing to do. Sara spread her beach towel on the grass near the town pool. The sun felt warm and inviting as she shed her tee shirt, shimmied off her jean skirt and kicked off her sandals. She sat down on the towel with a contented sigh, then slid onto her back. She should be slathering on the sunscreen—SPF 50, since it was her first exposure of the season—but decided to wait a few minutes. For now, she would stay right where she was, with her face up and her arms sprawled at her sides.

It felt good to be at the pool, even wearing last season's bathing suit. The faded one-piece held its shape, despite heavy use during the previous summer's trip to Conneaut Lake with the girls from work. She dreaded the thought of bathing suit shopping and compensating for any extra pounds she'd packed on since last Summer. But on this day, with blue skies and only one or two cotton clouds drifting by, she let herself simply sink into the serenity of the coming of summer. It wouldn't be long before she'd join the ranks of teachers everywhere who floated along on summer breezes.

Smiling, arms spread to catch every ray, Sara drifted into a light dream state. Even though she could hear the shouts of the children in the kiddie pool and the twang of the diving board each time a teenager did a cannonball into the main pool, she was in her happy place, away from her daily cares.

Soon enough she would pack up her classroom. She'd pull down the bulletin boards, the posters of the baby animals, the birthday chart—every last bit of paper flotsam that had made her classroom a temporary home for her kindergarten students this past year. She'd box up the books and wash the boards. It would be a welcome, calming ritual.

Then Sara's thoughts drifted over to the long, luxurious days of summer vacation. She hadn't done any planning, but that didn't bother her. She'd manage to fill each and every day. Although, by Last Memorial Day weekend, Jen, Charlotte and Sara had already developed the itinerary for a late-June sojourn to the lake cabin. It was strange that no one had brought up the subject of this year's trip during recent lunches.

Maybe there would be no trip this summer. Jen was preoccupied with the grade-changing hack and her possibly-blooming romance with Joe. Charlotte had Mitchell, and things were getting serious. Which could mean a wedding. Which could mean Sara as a—

Good God!

A bridesmaid!

She'd already played bridesmaid several times, with the astonishingly ugly gowns in the back of her closet to prove it. Might she even be matron of honor? She shuddered at the thought of that word, *matron*. But she knew she would look silly as a bridesmaid, all covered in flounces and ruffles. Maybe Char would allow her to attend the wedding as a humble guest. If so, who would be her plus-one?

Johnny?

That could get awkward. Weddings were minefields for romance—all the music and dancing and fancy clothes could get a girl's thoughts headed in the wrong direction.

If Jen and Joe became, well, *a thing*, Sara would be the only one of her circle of friends that didn't have a significant other. On one hand, it was good to know that she could take off anywhere at a moment's notice. On the other, she didn't have anyone to take off *with*.

This, she thought, *is pulling me out of my happy place.*

She needed to roll over on to her stomach and let the sun caress her back. With an unladylike grunt, Sara flipped over and mashed her face into the warm fabric of the beach towel. *Oh, yeah,* she thought, *this is what life is all about.*

Sara was drifting off to sleep when she became aware of cold, wet drops pinging onto her hot back. "What the…"

She twisted up into a sitting position, thinking rain had definitely not been in the forecast. A child stood over her. The youngster had clearly been in the pool only moments before because her hair was wringing wet and her juicy-fruit-striped two-piece bikini was sucked in close to her body.

Rebecca Swanson peered at Sara with the intensity of a hawk eyeing its prey. "Hi, Mrs. Goode!"

Sara tried hard to sound cheerful. "Hey, there, Rebecca." So much for the meditative state that might have healed her troubled soul. Sara reached for her beach bag and pulled out the sunscreen.

"I saw you when I was swimming, over there," Rebecca pointed in the direction of the pool.

"That's nice." Sara slathered on the lotion, avoiding eye contact with the classroom tattle-tale and hoping against hope that Rebecca would just leave. It was not that she disliked Rebecca exactly, she just found her...*trying.*

"No, Mrs. Goode," Rebecca said. She huffed in little-person exasperation.

Sara looked up at the girl and noticed that Rebecca's hands were on her hips in their accustomed tyrannical fashion.

"I was in the *big* pool! Not the kiddie pool with the babies. The big pool!"

"Oh...Welll... Good for you." Sara knew the girl was looking for high praise, but all Sara wanted to do was to go back to sleep.

"I'm a Flipper."

Sara felt compelled to ask. "And what's a Flipper?"

"That's me!" Rebecca giggled. "I took swimming lessons all winter and now I can swim in the big pool with the big kids. I can swim across the pool without drowning." Rebecca's eyes shone with pride.

Sara choked down her laughter. "Well," Sara said, "That's a very good thing, to be able to swim without drowning."

Rebecca twirled a strand of her wet spaghetti hair around her finger and then leaned in closer to her teacher. "You know, Mrs. Goode, I didn't tell nobody about that bad word that the boys said on the playground at school. Not even my mommy."

"Oh, Rebecca." Sara felt tempted to roll her eyes, so she slipped on her sunglasses. "Whatever am I going to do with you?"

"Nothing!" Rebecca giggled again. "'Cause I'm graduating from kindergarten next week!"

"Thanks for stopping by, Rebecca," Sara said firmly then slid down on to her back, preparing to sunbathe once again. "I'm going to go back to resting now."

"Okay. Bye, Mrs. Goode!" Rebecca took off in a spray of droplets paired with clumps of grass that her little feet kicked up as she returned to the vast pleasures of the big pool.

There were definitely hazards to living in the same town where one taught school. Sara ran into her students and their parents in the Giant supermarket, at the mall, and at the Eat 'n Park. Sara had to be on her best behavior at all times. She was a pillar of society, or so the teacher conduct handbooks inferred, a model of decorum, a virtual paragon of propriety.

Uh-huh, Sara thought to herself. *And monkeys might fly.* She might be a generally well-behaved and modest person, but she was capable of looking for and finding trouble. One had only to reference a couple of days ago when she had kissed Johnny in the Batmobile.

Things with Johnny were so...*complicated.* It would be simpler with someone new, someone who hadn't broken her heart all those years ago. Someone tall and blond, who would pull her into his strong arms and look deeply into her eyes for a few passionate seconds before bringing his soft, expressive lips to hers—

A shadow blocked the sunshine and stayed there. Then something touched Sara's nose.

Her eyes flew open, with her body braced for fight or flight.

There, crouched down beside her, was Bobby Moore, another soon-to-be-graduated kindergartner. Sara was going to have to find another swimming pool for her summer escapes.

"Hello, Bobby." Sara groaned as she struggled to sit up, her stomach muscles protesting the workout. She pulled off her sunglasses and squinted in the sunlight. "Wow. It's hot out, isn't it?"

"Yes, Mrs. Goode. The temperature is 95 degrees, and the humidity is 10 percent." Bobby had always seemed a boy of few words. Sara could always rely on Bobby to pass out papers, clean erasers, and pick up paper scraps from the classroom floor. As teachers often do, Sara had tried to imagine his future occupation and had come up with one clear winner—Bobby would be a policeman. He was so conscientious of right and wrong, but fortunately not in the bratty way that Rebecca was. Now, given his precise statements about the weather, she wondered if she should have assigned him a different career—like a meteorologist or even a lawyer.

"Who are you here with, Bobby?" Sara peered around the pool area, glancing at the gaggle of moms in lawn chairs, but didn't see Mrs. Moore anywhere. "Where's your mom?"

"I don't know where my mother is." Bobby's face took on a worried frown, and then he stood up fully and started to sway back and forth rhythmically on his little bare feet.

"Did she come with you today?" Sara asked, figuring that maybe another neighborhood mother had brought him along with her own children.

Bobby shook his head solemnly. "Nope."

As she tried to decide which of several obvious questions to ask next, Bobby interrupted her.

"Mommy went away. Now it's me and Daddy."

A little spark of fear ignited in Sara's chest. Was it divorce, or worse, death? Maybe Mrs. Moore had gone away on a solo vacation. She knew that sometimes marrieds felt the need to be alone. But Bobby was acting too upset for this to be just a mom's weekend away. Sara decided to tread very carefully. "Where did she go, Bobby?"

"We don't know, actually. Mommy just packed her stuff and went away. Daddy says we'll be okay."

Bobby looked at Sara with his big, trusting brown eyes, and all she could do was reassure him. "I'm sure Daddy's right. It will all work out." Sara smiled at him, and he gave her a tentative smile in return.

"Is your Daddy here?" Sara asked. She began scanning the crowd scattered at the poolside.

"Yes, he's over there," He turned around and pointed to the far side of the pool, an area shaded by trees.

Sara spotted Mr. Moore in a recliner, reading a hardcover book. At that moment, Mr. Moore looked up from his book and directly across the pool to Bobby and Sara. Clearly he had been keeping a regular eye on Bobby. Sara felt a heart tug as she gave a little wave to Bobby's dad.

Bobby saw his dad gazing at them, and started bouncing up and down, waving his arms and calling out, "Daddy! Daddy!" His voice carried over the pool area, causing many moms and a rare dad to turn in their direction.

Sara attempted to quiet Bobby, but it was too late. His dad got up and began to walk towards them. This day was just not going to give her the rest and relaxation she craved. She wanted to go home, grab a bag of Oreos and zone out in front of the TV, but she was curious about Bobby's family situation.

As Sara put on her professional smile, Bobby said, "Here comes Daddy."

Bobby's eyes were so bright; he clearly adored his father. Mr. Moore, Sara couldn't recall his first name, was a handsome man, but not in the traditional sense. He was of moderate height with wavy, thick dark hair that sometimes slipped down over his eyes. He was lean, but not thin, with the body of a runner or a swimmer. Sara remembered that on parents' night, last September, she was astonished at the size and strength of his hands as they shook hers in greeting. Sara noticed things like the grip of a man's hand. Such small details could be used to deduce the character of a person. Mr. Moore seemed like a solid, forthright man.

"Hey, there," Mr. Moore said to Sara as he came within speaking distance. "I hope this guy isn't bothering you too much." His eyes twinkled as he nodded towards Bobby.

"No, no. I don't know if you remember me, but I'm Sara Goode, Bobby's—"

"Teacher," Mr. Moore finished Sara's sentence, and continued with, "I never forget the people that are important in my child's life." He flashed Sara a megawatt smile.

Sara flushed to the roots of her hair. "Gee, that's a nice thing to say. I mean, to say that I'm someone important to Bobby…"

"Are you kidding? All he talks about is Mrs. Goode this, and Mrs. Goode that. You're his favorite person, hands down."

"After you, that is," Sara quickly added. She was a little uncomfortable with the accolades.

"Well, that's a given," he grinned immodestly.

Sara laughed in response then said, "I have to confess that I don't recall your first name, Mr. Moore. I only met you the one time, and I'm not that great with names. It takes me a week or two into the school year before I can name all the kids in my class. I make them wear name badges." Sara cringed. Was she talking too much? She was talking too much.

"No sweat. I'm David." And just like he did on parent's night, Mr. Moore reached out with both hands to shake hers.

A tremor of excitement ran through Sara when their hands touched. She wasn't sure why this was happening, but it felt warm and it felt right. She smiled, now openly glad to be in the sunshine, on the same stretch of grass as Bobby and David.

"It's a pleasure to meet you again…David." Sara emphasized his name. She wouldn't be forgetting it in the near future. Bobby watched closely, and Sara reminded herself that the boy had just lost his mother. In what fashion he had lost her, and for how long she would be gone, Sara didn't know. But it could only confuse Bobby if she jumped into the middle of all those unknowns. She pulled her hand from David's and cleared her throat. "Um, Bobby tells me that it's just you two bachelors at the pool today."

David's smile faded. For a long moment, he simply met her eyes, perhaps assessing how much to say. " Anna—my wife—left us a few weeks ago. She said she needed a change. So it's just me and Bobby. Mommy is divorcing us, right, big guy?" He addressed his son in a no-nonsense way, his voice firm and direct.

Sara flinched at the bare honesty. She wasn't sure that young children should be exposed to the intricacies of adult relationships, but teachers weren't supposed to judge.

"Anyway," said David, "it's a beautiful day, so we just had to celebrate summer with a jump in the pool."

"You didn't jump in the pool yet, Daddy," Bobby reminded his father.

"Guilty as charged. But I promise I will, Bobby."

Bobby gave a cheer, then told to Sara, "Dad and me are cooking a fire at our house when we get home. We're having burnt hot dogs and cherry pop!"

Sara laughed at his enthusiasm, and said, "Burnt hot dogs, huh? Those are the best."

David smiled, and said, "Obviously we're going to have a cookout with the grill. I'm not burning down the house, no matter what the kid says."

"I figured," Sara was thinking that burnt hot dogs sounded delicious right now.

"Hey, Dad. Can Mrs. Goode come over and have a hot dog, too?" Bobby grabbed on to his father's hand. "Please, Dad?"

David laughed again. "What kid wouldn't want his teacher over for a cookout?" He addressed Sara with an open look of approval.

"Actually, I think some of my students would rather have a tooth pulled than be seen with me out of school."

"Well, when the teacher is as pretty as you, I'm not going to call the dentist." David casually continued to look her over with his gentle brown eyes. "So?"

"Oh, no, no. I couldn't do that. You have plans. I couldn't impose, really," Sara didn't want to accept an invitation given because his son had a case of teacher-worship. Besides, she couldn't imagine crashing his cookout so soon after the loss of his wife. "Maybe some other time. A raincheck, okay?"

Bobby looked disappointed, but his father swept him up in his arms. "Hey, big guy, we'll just have to ask her again soon, okay? Maybe after you finish up with school, Mrs. Goode can come over for a barbecue." Sara watched the interaction between father and son with envy. She had wanted children, but it wasn't meant to be.

"We can build with my Legos!"

Sara nodded and gave a soft smile. "We'll see."

David Moore sensed Sara's reluctance and rallied by saying, "What are we waiting for, kiddo? Let's jump into that pool and let Mrs. Goode enjoy her day!" His words were a magic spell that set Bobby's feet flying.

"Last one in is a rotten egg!" Bobby called over his shoulder as he scampered towards the pool.

"Later, Sara," said David. Then he winked at her and turned to follow his son.

Sara wondered if she was perhaps too pleased that he remembered her first name. She was in no danger of forgetting his name any time soon.

CHAPTER FIFTEEN

"Why does the last day of school always have to be so flippin' hot?" Sara moaned as she ripped down the scalloped paper border from her classroom bulletin boards. Yards of the yellow and black trim coiled around the foot of the chair on which she was standing. The floor of her kindergarten classroom resembled the aftermath of a Super Bowl ticker tape parade in downtown Pittsburgh, long after the Steelers fans had gone home.

"I want to bask in the joy, not float away in a puddle of my own sweat." She gave one last yank to the remaining well-stapled border and threw the tangled result as far away from her as she could. It landed on her foot. "Oof. Done."

She stepped down, waded through the black and gold jungle, and slipped into her soft swivel chair. "Instead of the joy...I have the agony. The agony of sweat, the agony of smelling like..." She picked up her bottle of lukewarm water and chugged it straight down the bottom. "Like..." She swiveled her chair with her feet and tossed the plastic bottle across the room and into the grey industrial garbage can by the classroom door.

"Like a spoiled brat who can't take a little heat. By the way, ten points. Good shot." Jen had entered the classroom at the moment of Sara's bucket shot.

"Thanks. And, no, I am not a spoiled brat. However, I do think I'm beginning to stink like rotten eggs." Sara made another not-so-discreet attempt of smelling under her armpits. "Geez, I'm ripe. Really, I can't stand it." She rolled back over to her desk, and began emptying the drawers of a year's accumulation of chewed pencils, gooey white-out bottles and loose paper clips.

Jen shook her head impatiently. "Well, I promise you I didn't break the air conditioning in order to sabotage your last day of school. I didn't break it at all." She grabbed a red apple stress toy from Sara's junk pile. The PTA had given one to each of the staff on Teacher Appreciation Day in May. Much good it could do on a day like this, or any other day for that matter. Squeezing a spherical object did not de-stress Sara, it only reminded her how much she wanted to wring the necks of some of her students—and some of her co-workers.

Sara cocked her head at Jen. "Do I believe you, I wonder? Might not an employee with a twelve-month position want to take out her frustration on teachers who get the whole summer off?"

"Ha! I could care less whether you scammers get the whole summer off! Take off all of December, too, while you're at it. Oh, that's right. You already dooooo." Jen's cheeks began to grow red.

"Okay, okay. Stand down. I apologize. I really am sorry,-that was a low blow. I must be running on empty here. Friends?" She held out her arms, offering a hug.

Jen backed away. "Stay away from me, you freak. It's a hundred and one in here and you want body contact."

"So you *do* admit it's as hot as hell in here?"

"What? You think I haven't been suffering all day with the rest of you yahoos? And to top it off, I have the principal's hot, fetid breath down my neck every other minute." Jen struck a familiar "Principal Johnson" pose, something of a cross between a strutting rooster and a three-legged stray dog. "'Have you called the air conditioning company, Ms. Falcone?'" she asked in his nasal twang. "'Did you notify the school district, Ms. Falcone? Will the buses pick up the children earlier, Ms. Falcone?'" Jen grabbed fistfuls of her long dark hair. "I'm changing my name."

"I don't envy you. Here, let me make it up to you." She rummaged around in her bottom desk drawer. She palmed a small object into her hand and held the closed fist out to Jen. "This is for you."

Jen approached warily, "What is it?"

"Just take it. You'll like it, I promise."

"I don't trust you. I know you too well." She started a stare down with Sara, but Sara didn't break under the pressure. "Oh, okay, give it here."

Sara dumped the small prize into Jen's hand. Jen looked down and gasped. "A flicker ring? Is this a flicker ring?" She held the small silver ring up to her eyes and tilted it back and forth. "It is! Where did you get this? Look! First it's a Tonto then it's the Lone Ranger. Awesome!"

Sara laughed. "I got it on Ebay. I remember that you said you liked them when we had drinks at the Starlight Inn one night. It was a lucky find."

Jen ran over and hugged Sara from behind. "I don't care if it is hot in this room. Thank you, thank you, thank you!"

"You're welcome. Now get your sweaty body off of mine and let me finish cleaning out my desk. I'm going to have to do my student coverage in an hour, and I want most of this stuff done and out of the way before school lets out." The air conditioning in the school auditorium had fortuitously continued working due to a recent upgrade that had given the system separate wiring. The principal had declared June 8th an all-day Movie Day, much to the delight of the students. They had already watched *Finding Nemo* and were a half hour into the first *Ice Age.* Principal Johnson had also authorized a burger-and-fries delivery for lunch in the auditorium, so the kids were over the moon. Teachers were given rotating duty hours to alternately cover the students and break down their sweltering classrooms.

"Did you get any good gifts, Sara?" Jen pointed with her chin over to several gift bags on the window sill. Parents often gave teachers of the younger students tokens of appreciation at Christmas and at the end of the school year.

"I don't know. Want to open them for me?" Sara continued weeding out the junk and paraphernalia from her desk drawers. She'd already returned the small toys that she had collected from her students over the course of the year. Admittedly, she'd been a little reluctant to give back the Batmobile.

"Time? To open gifts? Why, of course!" Jen practically skipped over to the collection of bags with bright ribbons and tissue paper. "I told Mr. Johnson that I was going to the ladies' room. Let him think it's my time of month. He won't question it." She chose a bag covered in pink glitter and pulled out the white tissue. Inside was a small envelope. Jen opened it and read aloud, "'Dear Mrs. Goode, thank you for teaching my Tommy. He's going to miss you.' Aw, isn't that sweet. But, even better, here's a gift card to Barnes and Noble! You scored!"

"I did indeed."

Jen chose the next bag and pushed aside tissue paper to reveal an envelope and a white candle in a covered, glass jar. "The candle is called White Linen, and…" Jen opened the top to sniff, "It smells so fresh and clean."

"If you run across any boxes of chocolates, you can have them. I sure don't need them if I'm going to fit into my bathing suit this summer."

Jen said, "No chocolates—yet." She pointed to the remaining unopened gift bags. "But if I find some, you can't tell Joe. He's totally into this Penn-Jillete, Nutritarian stuff, and chocolate is not on the menu."

"Any candy in here is going to be soup at this point."

"Let's see who the candle came from," Jen ripped the envelope open and pulled out a folded note. She read aloud, "'Dear Mrs. Goode, it was a pleasure running into you at the pool last weekend. I hope you'll forgive my son for being so forward and asking you to dinner that evening. He's had a crush on you since the first day of school. I guess he gets his eagerness from his dad, because I'd like to ask you to join us for a BBQ at our house this coming Friday night. Again, it's fairly short notice, but I know Bobby would be thrilled. His dear old dad would like it as well. Send me an email. Sincerely, David Moore'"

As Jen lowered the note, Sara sat, open-mouthed. She had not expected to hear from David Moore again. Ever.

"How about that?" Jen said. "A candle and a date."

Sara ran her hands through her hair, sweat droplets scattering from her forehead. "No, no, no." She shook her head vehemently. "It's not a date, Jen. David Moore is just humoring his son. It means nothing."

"Hmm. Then why did Mr. Moore say that he would like you to come to dinner 'as well?'" Jen handed the note to Sara. "See? Right here."

"Stop insinuating something that isn't there. David Moore is a good father who is trying very hard to hold his family together since his wife left a few months ago. Little Bobby needs all the TLC he can get, considering that his mommy is gone. David probably wants to make Bobby as happy as he can, in spite of the tough situation." Sara took the note from Jen, folded it and placed it in her satchel on the floor.

"You do know we have a school policy about teachers dating the parents of their students?"

"As of three o'clock this afternoon, Bobby will no longer be my student."

"Okay, wise guy. Then how about not getting mixed up in someone else's troubles?" Jen said with true concern. "If I recall, the reason you came back to Pittsburgh was to nurse your own emotional wounds. Are you really ready to jump into the middle of another mess?"

"It's just a dinner, it isn't a shotgun wedding. I'll be fine." She hoped she sounded more confident than she actually felt. "Besides, it will make me feel a lot better if I can make the little guy forget his problems for a few hours."

Jen continued to stare at Sara.

"Really, Jen. Please support me with this," Sara said. "Remember I'm the one who gave you the flicker ring."

"What does that have to do with anything?"

"Well, anyone who buys you a flicker ring gets a free pass and collects two hundred dollars."

Jen sighed. "Fine. Go to your barbecue. You're a one-woman charitable institution, Sara."

"Yep. That's me." Sara nodded in agreement.

"But how are you going to do this barbecue and still have time to clean the house and get ready for your big party?"

"It's not my party. It's Nicky's and Gertie's party. It just happens to be at my house, and I just happen to be attending. Under duress, I'd like to add."

"Ah, don't be like that, honey." Jen started to rub her shoulders. "It will be loads of fun, and who knows? Maybe you'll meet someone tall, dark and handsome."

"Yeah, I've already done that and look how it worked out for me. One nasty divorce and a permanent distrust of the opposite sex."

"Ok. Then how about someone tall, blonde and handsome?"

"Johnny? You can stop trying to push us together."

"He kissed you in the Batmobile."

"I told you to never mention that!"

"It's just us here, Sara. So tell me, did you like it? Was it as good as you remembered?"

"No dice. You're not getting a peep out of me. When will I ever learn? Why did I ever have tell you in the first place?" Sara groaned and buried her head into her arms on her desk.

"Because we're besties, and this is what besties do," Jen stated matter-of-factly. "We spill."

"Huh-uh. Not this time. You know, Jen, maybe the past should stay in the past. I think Johnny is a great guy, but I just can't let go of my fears. I wish I could. I just don't know how."

Jen patted Sara's back. "I'm sorry, kid. I don't have any easy answers with this one. I wish I could wave my magic wand and make everything better."

"I know, Bestie," Sara gave a light punch to Jen's arm.

"I guess I'd better get back to the office. Principal Johnson is probably getting his boxer shorts in a twist without me there."

"No doubt. Hey, Jen, before you go. I know you've been crazy busy with end-of-the-year stuff, but I'm dying to know what happened with the hacking. How did Principal Johnson take it when you told him that it was his grandson who tampered with the online grade books?"

Jen tightened her lips. "It...didn't go so well. He just got quiet and sort of sat down—well, fell down—in his desk chair. He didn't say anything for a while, then he asked us to leave his office." Jen took a deep breath. "Joe and I were really nervous."

"I can imagine,"

"Then, after Joe had left, Principal Johnson called me back into his office."

"And?"

"Sara, you have to promise me that you'll keep this under wraps."

"You keep the Batmobile kiss quiet, and I'll keep this info on the down low."

"Okay, then. Principal Johnson dictated his resignation to me. I had to type it up and send a copy to all the members of the school board." Jen stared down at the floor tile. "Oh, Sara, it's the worst."

"Geez, Jen! I can't believe it. Did the school board accept his resignation?"

"I don't know, and he won't say anything about it. He just keeps carrying on as if everything is normal, but it's not! I don't want a new boss. He's been good to me." Jen blinked hard to hold back the impending tears.

"And he's been a good leader of this school. I can't believe he would leave because of something his grandson has done. Surely everyone will know that the computer hacking is not his fault."

"Principal Johnson has high standards of conduct. He thinks his family members are reflections of himself. Or, at least that's what he said in his letter to the board."

"I'm sorry, Jen. What a way to end the school year." Sara placed an arm around Jen's shoulder.

"No kidding." Jen pulled away and grabbed a tissue from a box on Sara's desk. "Anyway, I've got to go. Catch you later. And remember, mum's the word," Jen said firmly before leaving the classroom. Frowning, Jen held her flicker ring up and bounced her finger up and down to see the lenticular pictures. "Hi-ho, Silver, away!" she said weakly.

Sara sat back down at her desk. For a long time, she didn't pack anything else away. Suddenly, the end of the school year was not a time for celebration.

CHAPTER SIXTEEN

Sara rang the doorbell at 1010 Bluebell Lane, the home of David and Bobby Moore. She felt jittery as she stood on the doorstep, staring at the solid red door with the gold metal numbers. Was this a date, or was it just a thank-you dinner for the school teacher? She bounced from sandal to sandal, considering the options.

Earlier, she had gone through her entire wardrobe, trying to find the ideal outfit. However, not really knowing the purpose of the occasion led to a lot of guesswork. She finally decided on white capri pants with a white peasant top embroidered with multi-colored flowers. She felt girlish and a tad bohemian, hopefully inspiring a fun flirtation with David.

Sara remembered his dark, penetrating eyes and gave a little shiver of anticipation. David was cute, in a middle-class, Mr. Clean and All-American way. She didn't generally go for the average good-looking guys, but she was certainly more than a little attracted to David. Her previous romantic entanglements with men like handsome Johnny or her macho-man ex-husband hadn't been successful, so getting to know a normal man seemed like a fine idea.

Sara frowned then rang the doorbell a second time. Did she have the right time? Was it the right day? Yes, of course, she was there at the correct time. She'd checked the invitation right before she left her apartment. She'd been invited for a barbecue dinner at 6 p.m.

Sara stepped back from the door and attempted to peer through the living room window. Fluffy white curtains marred her view through the glass. There didn't appear to be any lights on in the room.

Just as Sara stepped back to the door and raised her hand for her third and final knock, the red door flew open, startling Sara and causing her to exclaim, "Oh!"

In the foyer, David stood with his hand over a cell phone and whispered a severe "Shhh!"

Sara pointed to herself quizzically, and David nodded emphatically.

"Ex-wife's lawyer." David whispered again. Then continuing the conversation with the person on the other end of the phone, he said, "No. You listen to me! I will not pay any support to a woman who deserted her own child!"

While he closed the front door, David waved Sara into the house and pointed towards the living room. Sara took that to mean she was to find a seat while David continued with his negotiations. She gingerly shuffled her feet into the darkened room as her eyes adjusted to the lack of light. She stepped on something squishy, but bravely kept moving towards a large shape that she hoped was a couch.

It was indeed a couch, unfortunately covered in newspapers, empty cracker boxes and unopened mail. Sara gently pushed a mountain of paper to one side and slid into the small space she had excavated from the mess. As she gingerly sat down, and her eyes began to adjust to the low light, she began to make out other shapes throughout the room. It seemed that the living room floor and end tables had become a dumping ground for old pizza boxes, empty shoe boxes and Pop Tart wrappers.

Sara felt queasy. She wondered if David was a hoarder, like those obsessed people on TV who couldn't throw away old Christmas trees and decades of *National Geographic* magazines.

Her eyes slid from the paper-strewn room to David himself, as he stood in the foyer, talking loudly into his cell phone. He looked normal, so clean and put together. It didn't seem possible that a respectable person could live in these conditions, but there he was, in the hallway just outside of ground zero.

Sara closed her eyes and took a deep breath. Maybe his cleaning woman had missed a few days this week? Or maybe David was too preoccupied with Bobby and the contentious divorce—or his challenging job—to be able to focus on cleaning. Still, he really should keep the house clean for Bobby, if not for himself.

Bobby. Yes, where was Bobby?

Sara shot up and picked her way over to David. She mouthed, "Where's Bobby?"

David pointed at the stairs just down the hallway, and whispered, "Up in his room."

Sara nodded, pointed to herself and then to the stairs for permission to go up.

David ignored her and stomped away, shouting, "I won't discuss this any further without my lawyer present! There will be no alimony, and I sure as hell won't be dividing any property!"

Sara, embarrassed, tiptoed to the stairs and climbed to the second floor, avoiding small metal trucks with wheels and electronic creatures with sharp legs and antennae. "Bobby?" she called softly.

She walked past the master bedroom, with sheets balled up at the end of the king size bed, and various tee shirts, boxer shorts and running shoes scattered around the floor. She found Bobby in his bedroom, sitting on the carpeted floor, at least ten thousand pieces of Lego surrounding him. It was an odd picture, considering that Bobby had been the one child who made it his mission to keep her classroom neat and clean. But in fact, the rest of his room was neat and highly organized, with books on the shelves and other toys stowed in a large wood box. The oddness of the Legos scattered all over the floor while the rest of the room was in perfect order puzzled Sara. She understood that Bobby would want to have some order in his life, considering the departure of his mother, his father's apparent anger at the situation and the horrid mess inside the house. The Legos must be the one area where Bobby let himself become free and creative, where he didn't have to maintain control over the chaos.

Bobby was focused intently on building some sort of vehicle, based on a picture on the Lego package. He didn't notice her come into the room.

"Hi, Bobby!" she called. Startled, Bobby looked up then gave a shout as he saw her. "Mrs. Goode! You're here! Daddy said you'd come!" Bobby leaped up and threw himself into Sara's arms.

"Oof! I'm glad to see you, too, kiddo, but easy on my stomach. I'm going to need it later for dinner."

Bobby let go and grinned up at Sara. "Sorry, Mrs. Goode. I didn't mean to hurt you. I'm excited, that's all."

"No harm done. Now let's use that energy with your Legos, okay? What are you making?" Sara slid down to the floor, brushing piles of plastic blocks away to clear an area to sit.

"I'm making a spaceship." He gazed forlornly around at the scattered Lego pieces. "But I don't know how to do it, and Daddy said he can't help me. He said to try to do it myself. Mommy used to help me all the time. Before she had to leave."

Sara said, "Oh, I'm sure your Daddy wants to help you. He's just busy right now." She knew how much Bobby meant to David. He wouldn't purposely shrug off an opportunity to spend quality time with his son.

Bobby shook his head. "Nope. I don't think so. He said he doesn't want to waste his time playing with Legos. So I'm pretty sure that means 'no.'"

Sara's eyes widened in surprise.

"I'll play with you. For a while, anyway, until Daddy gets dinner ready."

Sara wondered what type of man David actually was. Bobby clearly adored David, and was well-taken care of, but Sara was starting to doubt that David was the model father he had seemed to be at the local swimming pool.

Sara noticed a shelf over Bobby's bed lined with superhero action figures. "Hey, Bobby. Who's your favorite superhero?"

"I like Ant-Man."

"Really?" Sara asked in mild surprise. "I was sure you were going to say Spider-Man or Superman."

"Nah," said Bobby. "All the other kids like them, but not me."

"Why do you like Ant-Man?"

"Cause he can get small, like me. Then he can go places and do stuff and people don't see him." Bobby returned to scanning his Lego pile. "He's way cool."

Sara smiled, and said, "You know, Bobby, you're pretty cool yourself."

Bobby grinned and said, "Thanks." He snapped a plastic piece on to his slowly-forming spaceship. "I know who your favorite superhero is, Mrs. Goode. It's Batman."

Sarah gulped and pretended to be studying the illustrations on the Lego box. "Goodness, you're right, Bobby. How did you know?"

"Well, every time you want us kids to be good, you tell us to do the right thing and be like Batman. So that's how I know you like Batman."

"Exactly right," Sara replied. She realized that anything she might say as a teacher might be remembered and interpreted by a child as bright and sensitive as Bobby.

"Mrs. Goode, can I tell you a secret?" Bobby whispered his question and scooted in closer to Sara.

"Uh, um, yeah, sure, go ahead."

"When Mommy left, she told me she's going to come back and get me. But I can't tell Daddy 'cause it's a secret." Bobby smiled up at Sara with trusting eyes.

"Is that what you want, Bobby?" Sara asked in a low voice. "For Mommy to come back and get you?"

"Yep. But it sure is taking a long time. Waiting is hard."

Sara reached over and patted Bobby's hand. "Hang in there, Bobby. Your mommy is probably working as hard as she can to do the right thing." Sara's heart melted to think of the strain that her young student must be experiencing while he kept his secret and waited for his mother. She wished that there was something that she could do, but she knew better than to get involved. The Moores were relative strangers to her.

She spent maybe thirty, forty minutes, though it seemed like hours, searching through the brightly-colored bricks for pieces that matched the illustration. They had managed to add a handful to the spaceship, with many more to go, when Sara began to get suspicious. Was she babysitting Bobby, while David continued to rant downstairs?

Come to think of it, she hadn't actually heard David in the last five minutes. Maybe she should go and see what had become of him.

"Bobby, I'm going downstairs and see if I can help with dinner, okay?"

Disappointment clouded his sweet face, but answered, "Okay, I guess."

Sara rubbed his head affectionately took care making her way out of the room. One wrong step on a plastic block would send her ankle twisting in a very wrong position. Downstairs, she found that David was no longer in the foyer and didn't answer when Sara called his name. She explored and found the kitchen. She wasn't at all surprised to see that the sink was overflowing with dirty dishes. She considered making an escape from the house, but then heard David's voice through the screen door to the back yard.

Outside, David stood gazing over the hedge at his next door neighbor, a luscious blonde with extremely large breasts. A wave of disappointment washed over Sara. She had thought this was a date. She had thought there was an attraction between herself and David. But here he was, flirting with this bimbo while Sara babysat his child.

Sara pretended to clear her throat.

David quickly swiveled his head towards her, seeming surprised to see her there. "Oh, hi, Sara. I thought you were upstairs with Bobby."

"I was. But now I'm down here."

David blinked and smiled awkwardly. "And so you are." He gestured toward the blonde. "Tiffany, I'd like to introduce you to Bobby's kindergarten teacher, Sara Goode. Bobby invited her over for a barbecue to celebrate the end of the school year. He sure loves his teacher."

Tiffany—of *course* her name was *Tiffany*—moved her warm gaze from David and surveyed Sara head to toe. Her face said she felt no threat from this schoolteacher. She gushed, "Oh, isn't that darling. Lord knows, you poor school teachers really do deserve to be treated extra special for all your hard work."

Sara ignored Tiffany. She was too busy parsing David's claim that she was *Bobby's* guest. David was acting as if he had absolutely nothing to do with Sara's being here. Something smelled foul, and it wasn't the empty pizza boxes in the living room.

David said, "I was filling Tiffany in with the latest crap about my ex. She's been so supportive in this difficult time." He grinned, staring at Tiffany's generous cleavage as he said this.

"I'm sure she has been," said Sara through gritted teeth. Then, putting on her sweetest smile, "David, is there anything I can do to help with dinner? Any salad to prepare, veggies to cut up?"

David waved a reluctant goodbye to Tiffany and gestured to Sara to follow him. "Hungry? I have the grill all fired up, and we should be ready to eat soon."

Sara tossed a glance in the direction of the grill, where she saw no evidence of cooking meat. She gave a slight sigh as she realized that it was going to be a long evening.

"Hey, you're not getting tired, are you?" David said. "I want you to meet the girls!"

"Girls?" Sara knew that Bobby was an only child. Perhaps David had invited other women to this shindig. With the weirdness that she'd experienced since her arrival, Sara would not have been surprised to see two Playboy Bunnies walk out of the house. Instead, David steered her towards a thick metal fence with a secured, swinging door. He rattled at the chains that held the fence closed, and within seconds the sound of aggressive barking filled the yard.

Sara stepped back from the now-unlocked and open door.

"You're not afraid of dogs, are you?" asked David.

She tried to answer that she had a dog at home, but couldn't get a word in between the barks and growls, which were growing louder and more ferocious. Suddenly, two large German Shepherds appeared running at full speed, right towards Sara.

She screamed, loud and long, and didn't stop screaming until the dogs were standing on their hind legs and knocking her backwards. Sara fell hard on her back to the ground, the wind completely knocked out of her. The dogs gave a few sloppy wet licks to her face then returned to their compound as David yelled and yanked at their collars.

Sara lay in the dust, wheezing and gasping for air. She was terribly afraid that she'd broken a bone or two. It wasn't until David hovered over her grinning, that she attempted to move.

"Hey, now, sorry about that," he said. "The girls are so friendly, and they just wanted to meet you." He reached out his hand for Sara to grasp, and he pulled her up in one swift motion. "See?" he said. "No harm done."

As Sara slowly moved her arms and legs, she couldn't help but notice that dirt covered the front of her pants and her peasant blouse. She could only imagine what she looked like from behind.

"That's being friendly? You've got to be kidding." Sara tried to keep her voice calm, but a little hysteria threaded through. "Look at me; I'm filthy. David, I need to go home and change."

David laughed. "Of course, you don't! What's a little dirt with your dinner?" He began batting at her filthy clothing until Sara pushed his hands away.

"A little dirt?" she muttered under her breath as she swiped at the dust on her clothing. "It looks like I fell into a mud hole." David either ignored or didn't hear her comments.

"I'm going in to get the meat for the grill. Why don't you sit down at the picnic table?" He pointed across the yard to a warped table, gray from weathering.

As Sara gingerly sat down, David came through the kitchen screen door, holding aloft a large white plate. As he passed her on the way to the grill, Sara saw two huge hunks of steak and a hot dog on the plate. She could tell by the thickness of the steaks that it was going to be some time before dinner was served. David placed the meat on the flaming grill, and passed her again on his way to the kitchen. "I'll get Bobby and some clean plates."

Sara sat, pensive and alone. She was hoping that David had put together some tasty sides, like a fresh salad or baked beans, to accent the meal. She had really worked up an appetite in the last hour. Good food would go a long way in her ability to forgive David for all of the slights and injuries she had suffered since she had arrived.

David reemerged from the kitchen with Bobby in tow. David carried a stack of dishes, and some knives and forks. Bobby had several paper napkins crumpled in his fists. They set the table, and Sara complimented Bobby for helping his dad. David walked over to the grill, piled the meat back on a plate and carried it over to the table. "Dinner is served," he said.

Sara thought he was pulling her leg. He had cooked the steaks for maybe ten minutes, at the most. And where were the side dishes? But as David sat across the table from her, speared a hunk of barely cooked steak on to her plate, and then did the same for himself, she realized this was no joke. There would be no potato salad tonight.

David placed Bobby's hot dog on his plate. "Dig in!" he said joyfully.

Sara stared at her steak. The meat was lightly cooked on the outside; she didn't have to see the inside to know it was raw. She took her knife, and cut into the meat anyway. Blood splashed out and on to her already dirt-stained shirt.

She looked across the table to see David spearing a piece of oozing steak and thrusting it into his mouth. She swallowed the bile that rose in her throat.

"Um, David? I was wondering if you could cook my steak a little longer?" She gave him a weak smile. "I'm afraid that this is too rare for me."

David looked at her in surprise. "Really? Because this is the way I cook it, and I like it."

"Well, sure, if that's the way you like it. But I really need my meat to be cooked all the way through," Sara said.

Bobby laughed and said, "Yeah, Dad, she can't eat the cow if it's still mooing!"

David, exasperated with her request, reached for her plate, stood up and walked over to the grill. "Steak Tartare is considered a delicacy," he said. He dumped the steak on to the hot rack then returned to savagely chew on his own piece of raw beef. Sara tried to remain calm and looked away from David, pretending to be interested in the yard. She considered asking for something to drink, but she didn't want to trifle with David's crabbiness.

It was while she was looking at anything else but her graceless host that she foresaw impending doom. The two German Shepherds were edging towards the swinging door of their enclosure. Instantly, Sara realized that David hadn't re-chained it and that the dogs could escape by merely pushing it. She stood, pointed to the dogs, and began to yell, but it was too late for any remedial efforts. The dogs shot through the doorway and across the yard to the grill. With no fear of the heat, one of them snatched Sara's steak from the grill. The other made a grab for it from her sister's mouth, and they growled and tumbled over each other as they fought for possession of the meat.

They were snapping. They were snarling. They were rolling right toward the table. They had bloodlust in their eyes, they had murder. Within seconds, they would be in the laps of the three humans— three alternate sources of rare, red meat.

In a blind panic, Sara grabbed David's steak right off his plate and threw it as far as she could across the yard. She pulled Bobby from his bench and cried, "Come on, Bobby, run!" She held his hand and tore, half-dragging the child, toward the kitchen door. Surely she had broken some Olympic record for speed.

Once inside, she turned to see that the dogs had set upon David's steak like two ferocious beasts from hell. David was still sitting at the table, his eyes round in shock.

Sara didn't have to think of her next move. She ran wildly through the house with Bobby, her heart beating in her chest. She leapt over errant plastic blocks and empty bottles of chocolate milk. In no time, she and Bobby were at the front door. "Bobby, go to your bedroom and shut your bedroom door. Go, now!" Bobby ran as fast his sneakers could take him up the stairs to his bedroom.

Sara flew down the sidewalk and into her parked car. She pulled her cell phone from the glove compartment and dialed 911 with shaking fingers. The dogs might be sated by the hunks of meat they had just swallowed, but she couldn't take a chance. "Dog attack at 1010 Bluebell Lane. Please hurry!"

After giving some further identifying information, she clicked off her phone and threw it into her purse. She heard the sounds of police sirens in the distance and knew that help was on its way, whether it was needed or not. She started her car and drove a few houses down the street to give the emergency vehicles room to park in front of the Moore home. She rested her head against the steering wheel and took deep cleansing breaths to settle her trembling.

No bones about it—David was a freak.

Sara began to have an inkling why his wife had left and hoped that she would return for Bobby in the near future. Hopefully, at a minimum, the soon-to-be-ex Mrs. Moore would get visitation rights so that Bobby could have a half-way normal childhood. That was assuming she was competent—a tough call, since she had married a psycho like David.

Sara's foray into the dating world was a total disaster. It would be hard to bounce back from a nightmare of this magnitude. She wasn't even sure she wanted to try. As she watched the police cars drive down the street and stop in front of the Moore residence, she decided it was best to head home. She would hate to have to face David Moore after he saw the police come streaming through his door. Her work here was done.

CHAPTER SEVENTEEN

Sara hugged her favorite pillow close to her face. It felt so nice and cool and... *what?* What was that sound? It must have been the same sound that just woke her. She listened carefully for a few seconds, realized that she was hearing the awkward turning of a key in her front door. Her heart leapt into her throat, as she lay frozen on her bed, fearing the unimaginable. Someone was breaking into her apartment. But how did they have a key? And where was Dog? Shouldn't he be barking his little head off? For a few terrifying moments more, she heard nothing. Then, there was the distinct sound of her front door closing.

Sara threw her sheets to the side and jumped off the bed. She looked wildly around the room and grabbed her lamp from the night table. She would do whatever she had to do to survive. She raised the lamp, with its ruffled lamp shade, high above her ahead, waiting for the moment when the intruder came close enough that she could smash it on his head. Footsteps, muffled by the carpet, slowly came towards her. She could barely breathe as she lifted the lamp higher, her only advantage the element of surprise. She saw a leg clear the doorway, a man's running shoe and then...

"Sara! Where the heck are you?" A voice boomed out in the relative darkness of her bedroom. With her shades pulled down, it was difficult to make out even the outline of the intruder.

It took every bit of restraint Sara had not to fling the lamp as she saw the man's face.

It was Joe.

Sara doubled over in relief, gasping in air by the lungful. Adrenaline still coursed through her body like liquid lightning.

She returned the lamp to the night table and collapsed on to her bed. She pulled the sheets over her nightgown in a haphazard fashion. Dog jumped up onto her duvet and began licking his paws, but Sara didn't have the energy to make him get off.

"Joe! What are you doing here? Why were you sneaking in? I almost had a heart attack, dammit! You scared the hell out of me!"

In response, Joe gave a clownish smile. He looked more satisfied than concerned, more like a cat who had just eaten a particularly scrumptious bird.

"You're made of sterner stuff than that," Joe said. "Remember the time that Lexus side-swiped you in the crosswalk, and you tried to pull the driver out with your bare—?"

"*How did you get in here?!*"

"Sara, don't you remember you gave me a copy of your key ages ago?"

"That key was supposed to be used in the event of an emergency, you numbskull! Not on a Saturday morning when everything is fine, and I haven't had my coffee yet!" She pushed wild strands of hair out of her eyes. "Why didn't you just knock like a normal person?"

"I did. I swear! But you didn't answer so I decided to use the key."

"I don't like strange men coming uninvited into my bedroom. This is creeping me out." She watched Dog burrow into the bedding at the end of her bed. "And you, Dog, are worthless. Not one bark out of you. I could have been in big trouble here, and then who would have given you yummy dog treats?"

Joe stepped over and attempted to scratch Dog's head through the covers. He wound up scratching his hind leg. "Dog knows me. He knows I'm one of the good guys."

"So this is the famous boudoir of Sara Goode." He looked around in mock awe. "Frilly white curtains, white chenille bedspread—you need some accent colors, like bright pink and lime green sashes on the curtains. You could also get some pillow shams. They have a nice pink and green paisley pattern at Bed, Bath and Beyond. And—"

"How are you not gay?"

Joe sat down next to Dog on the end of the bed. "I'm blessed with being both wildly heterosexual and a whiz at design."

"Lucky for Jen. She won't have to choose her linens alone anymore, will she?"

"Not if I have anything to say about it!"

So Joe liked the idea of decorating a house with Jen...

"So why are you here? Have you proposed to Jen in a fit of passion?"

Joe's smile faded and he stammered. "No, not that. Er, not yet, anyway." He cleared his throat. "I actually stopped by to see how last night's date went. You know, with Bobby's father."

"Oh, Bobby's father. Yeah, David Moore. I had forgotten about last night over the excitement of nearly killing you with a lamp." She was still holding the lamp. She wasn't sure what to do with it, actually. And now Joe had re-awakened her embarrassment from last night. "Joe, it was an epic disaster."

"Oh, come on, how bad could it be?"

"Well, let's see: First, David spent about an hour on the phone with his soon-to-be ex-wife's lawyer—while I played Legos with Bobby. When he stopped yelling at the lawyer, did he come get me? No! I had to go hunting, and found him flirting over the back fence with the bombshell Lolita from next door. Finally, he served me a steak so raw that it still had a pulse, and expected me to eat it. And... and...and..." She shuddered. There was almost too much to tell. "I called the police, Joe."

"Because the dogs started to attack?"

"Yes!" she exclaimed. "It was like something out of a Stephen King novel. The German Shepherds broke out and stole my steak right off the grill. They tore it to shreds—and tried to tear each other to shreds along the way! I thought they were headed for the table—and I just knew they'd come through *us* to do it—so I threw David's steak into the yard. Then I—Wait... how did *you* know about the dogs?"

"Huh?" Joe's look of innocence was pure bluff.

"The dogs, Joe! Who told you about the dogs?" Dog lifted his sleepy head at the mention of his name, but sunk back down when Sara ignored him to glare at Joe.

Joe's face went pale. Pal*er*. "Now, Sara, sweetie, I want you to calm down. There's something I have to show you, and you can't be at DEFCON 2 before you see it." He reached around to his back pocket and pulled out a newspaper.

"This morning's paper, hot off the presses." He handed it over.

Sara scanned the front page as Joe said, "It's on page two."

On page two, her eyes immediately went to the headline below the fold. LOCAL MAN'S DOGS JOIN BBQ.

"Nooo," she whispered. "How did this get in the paper?"

"It seems a reporter was listening in to the police radio band when they got the call about two attacking dogs. He was on the scene in time to interview the cops and get a picture. Uh, David declined to comment."

Sara squinted at the grainy photograph to the right of the article. She saw David, talking to a uniformed police officer. In the background were various emergency response vehicles.

"This is bad," moaned Sara. "This is very bad." She flung the paper down and hugged her arms around herself. She was shaking slightly. "David must have been mortified. I hope they didn't take his dogs or anything."

Joe reached for the paper, picked it up and quietly looked through article. "It says here that the owner of the dogs was given a citation for not having the dogs on a chain or in a pen. In David's defense, it appears that the dogs had escaped their kennel, and it was all a misunderstanding."

Sara bit at a nail. "Am I mentioned in the article, by any chance?" she asked nervously.

"Um, let's see. No. It just says that the incident was reported by an unidentified caller to 911. You're off the hook!" Joe seemed to be trying to resurrect Sara's mood.

It wasn't working. "Oh my god, what about Bobby? He's going to be traumatized. His teacher runs away when the dogs attack, and the police rush in with all the bells and lights on."

Joe moved closer to Sara and patted her hand. "Not to worry, Sara. If I'm not mistaken, there's a little kid sitting in the front seat of the fire truck. Look! Bobby wasn't traumatized, he was ecstatic!"

"Let me see." Sara ripped the paper from Joe's hands and viewed the photograph. "Okay, could be…No, I think you're right! That definitely looks like Bobby. Oh, thank goodness." She sighed with enormous relief as Joe added, "No doubt he'll have that memory for the rest of his life."

"So will his dad," she said morosely.

"From the things you've said about last night, he had some bad karma coming after the way he treated you."

Sara offered a weak smile. "As I've told you before, I'm not very good at this dating thing. I should just go back to stalking Adam West."

Joe stood up and replaced the newspaper in the back pocket of his jeans. "Well, you better get cracking, sister, because tonight's the main event." He started announcing like a ringmaster at a circus. "The party to end all parties! Will Sara find that one special man?" Then in a quieter tone, he said, "This is all a bit nuts, isn't it?"

"Of course, it's nuts! How did I let everyone railroad me into this? I'm past my prime, past this whole dating scene." She sighed. "Are you coming? Are you bringing Jen?"

"Yes and yes. I'm also bringing a coworker who's been in town this week working on my company's latest contract. I'm meeting this guy for lunch, and then I figured he could enjoy himself here before going back to Connecticut. I hope you don't mind."

"There are going to be so many people here, one more won't make a difference. What's his name?"

"Sam. He seems like a nice enough guy."

"That's what they all are on the surface, until you get to know them," Sara pouted.

"I'm not a complete failure, and I'm an educated, technological prodigy," Joe extended his arms in a grand flourish.

Sara had a brief flash of a thought. "You know, Joe. There's something you might be able to do for me. Consider it partial payback for breaking and entering into my home."

"Spill it. I'm not committing to anything until I hear the details."

"I'm sure Jen has told you about Principal Johnson's resignation."

"Maybe, maybe not. Such information would be confidential."

"Yes, but when two people are in love, nothing stays a secret, so don't play coy. Here's the deal: I need you to talk to Principal Johnson and explain how young kids today aren't aware of all the social rules that go with computers. Things like confidentiality. And respect for others. Kids are handed these powerful technological tools but they don't have the wisdom or the maturity level to understand the responsibilities that go with that power. Tell him that his grandson can learn a lesson from his experience. The boy needs to be given the opportunity to understand the consequences of his actions. And, one of those consequences doesn't need to be his grandfather walking away from his job. Wouldn't it send a better message to the school community if the Principal took this debacle and turned it into an educational lesson? This goes right along with all those behavior programs that the district is always asking us to follow. I think the Principal needs to see this situation from a different point of view, and I think you're the one to show him."

"Yeah, I'm sure Principal Johnson sees me as a trusted advisor on his career and personal issues. "

"That's the point, Joe. It shouldn't *be* a personal issue. He should see this computer hacking as a sign of what's needed in the curriculum. He could even create a whole new program for the entire school district. You see? A negative into a positive!"

Joe groaned and rolled his eyes. "This isn't going to be easy."

"Nothing worthwhile ever is."

"Fine! I'll give it a try, but no promises, Sara."

"That's all I'm asking. Now that we are in agreement, I'd like to see the back of you heading out my front door." She slid out of the bed with the sheet still covering her. "I have to get this house ready for the party, and then Mom wants me to help with some baking."

"Baking? Who bakes for a party? Toss some cheese puffs into a bowl, and *voila*, you're ready!"

Sara herded him out of bedroom and into the hallway with a pillow applied repeatedly to his head and shoulders.

As he opened the front door, she said, "One more thing, Joe?" She held out her hand, palm up. "Give me back my key."

"Sara, really?"

She just glared.

Defeated, Joe reached into his pants pocket, pulled out his key ring and removed the key to Sara's front door.

Sara accepted it, adding. "If you go and talk to Principal Johnson, you can have this back," she said.

He stepped glumly out the door, turned, and opened his mouth to say something else.

Sara closed the door in his face.

CHAPTER EIGHTEEN

Sara had just stepped out of a refreshing shower when she heard furious knocking on her kitchen door. She ran barefoot across the living room, her wet feet making impressions in the carpet.

At the kitchen door, she said, "Hello?"

Johnny's voice answered. "Sara, open up. I need to talk to you."

She unlocked and opened the door. "What's going on?" she asked as he hurried in. "Is everything okay?" She stood back, repositioning her bath towel.

His forehead wrinkled with a frown, and he rubbed his jaw roughly with his hand.

"Uh—Why don't you get dressed or something first? I'll wait here. Sorry I caught you at a bad time." Johnny offered a sideways smile of chagrin. Sara briefly hesitated; she didn't want him to have to wait if he had something urgent to say. However, common sense won out. She felt chilled, and water was dripping down her legs.

"Okay. Be back in just a few minutes. Go ahead and start a pot of coffee."

"I'll be fine. Take your time." She noted that Johnny spoke calmly yet he made no eye contact, creating an invisible barrier between them.

Sara ran to her bedroom, towel-dried her hair then tossed on underwear, a white tee shirt and jeans. She grabbed her hairbrush from the bathroom, then walked back to the kitchen, briskly brushing through the tangles and knots in her wet hair.

Johnny was still standing, hands in pockets, eyes cast downcast to the floor.

"Okay, Johnny, what's going on?"

When he spoke, he spoke slowly. "I need…" He hesitated mid-sentence then gave a huge sigh, as if the weight of the world rested on his broad shoulders. "What I mean to say is, I …" Again he stopped himself.

Sara became alarmed asked him to sit down at the kitchen table. She sat across from him, her hands folded on the table. "What is it, Johnny?" She asked softly.

Johnny took one deep cleansing breath, and then said, "Sara, I can't come to this party that you and your family are having tonight. Joe told me the real reason behind it, and it makes no sense to me. Why do you need to have a party to meet a bunch of men from all over the Pittsburgh area, when there are plenty of guys ready and willing to date you right here in Brighton Park?"

So the idea of her meeting men was bothering him. Was she surprised? Maybe.

"Johnny, the party wasn't my idea, and I'm certainly not in charge of it. I agreed to go along with it because it means so much to my family and friends. They want me to get out there and start meeting new people."

She was avoiding the essential question, and she knew it.

"What about your old friends?" he asked. "Don't we get any consideration?" He opened his hands and held them towards her. His blue eyes met hers, and she felt a warmth enter her heart.

Sara tried to shake her confusion from her head. "You're invited to the party."

"No, Sara. That's not enough." He gently took her hands into his grasp. "You need to give me a fair chance."

"But…" Sara stumbled over her words. "I told you I would. I just need more time."

"You did. But I don't see how having a party to meet new men is giving me a fair shake."

Sara felt a wave of embarrassment sweep over her. Johnny was right. She hadn't stopped to look at the consequences of this party. She had wanted to please her sister and friends, but she hadn't stopped to consider Johnny's feelings.

Johnny interrupted her thoughts. "I can't help thinking that you want to ignore me. Do you want me to go away, Sara?"

"Go away?" Sara softly asked.

"I mean, do you want me to leave you alone? I know better than to hang around where I'm not wanted."

"Johnny, we've been such good friends since I've come back. I don't want to ever lose that. I *do* have feelings for you. They...go beyond friendship, and they scare me."

"Scare you? Don't you think I've proven myself over this last year?"

"You've been wonderful to me," Sara said. "I just need more time."

"For what? To see if you can trust me? To see if I'm a man of my word?" Johnny's voice began to rise in frustration. "This is it, Sara. This is me. I can do nothing more than I already have to show you how much I care and how much I want you in my life."

"I know that, Johnny," Sara stammered. She didn't want this confrontation right now. Too much craziness already filled her life. Couldn't she just have one day where she could breathe and not have to think about relationships? Couldn't she have the time she needed to heal before moving on?

"Have I been reading you wrong?" Johnny leaned in towards her, his intense blue eyes meeting hers directly. There could be no mistaking the hurt in his eyes and the pleading in his voice. He gently added, "I've felt the connection; I've seen how you can be with me."

"I've been trying to let things happen naturally. With us. With our friendship," Her eyes brimmed with tears. "Sometimes I feel sparks, like on the day we rode in the Batmobile. It was such a wonderful time, really," She looked away abruptly. "But sometimes I'm not sure that any of it is real. It feels too good to be true, and I've been through that before."

Sara needed to be certain of her feelings before she could even begin to express any genuine affection to Johnny.

"Johnny, you've grown to be one of my closest friends. I cherish that, and I don't want to lose you again. I'm afraid that if we rush into something, a relationship, we may destroy everything we've been building since I returned home." Her words felt hollow in her ears.

"You have to know that I would never hurt you again the way I did when we were younger, Sara. I need you to believe that."

Sara grabbed his wrists. "I *do*, Johnny. I do believe you. It's just that I'm not ready to trade our friendship for something more complicated. At least, not right at this minute. I know that's not the answer you're looking for, but it's all I have for now."

He pulled away his hands. "Sara, I'm not sure I can wait anymore."

"I would never put limitations on you. But if you start dating other men, I don't think I can handle it. What do you think that that says to me?"

Sara's hot tears rolled down her cheeks. She shook her head sadly.

"I would like to stay your friend, Sara. But I don't think I can manage that under these circumstances. I can't be near you if you're with someone else."

"That's it, then?" Sara said, barely able to hear her own voice. "Because I do need more time… and space. I need to really take a look at where I am and what I want from my life. I got married much too quickly, so I have to be smarter this time. I have to really know what's going to make me happy." She stopped and met his eyes in a long gaze. "I care about you, Johnny. And I want us both to find happiness, whether it's together or apart. But rushing things is definitely not going to help the process."

She took a deep breath to steady her nerves. "Please don't walk away."

The muscle in his jaw tightened as he stared into the morning sunlight.

"Let me think about it."

"Can we still be friends until you decide?"

Johnny pushed his chair away from the table and stood up. "Come here and give me a hug," he said brusquely.

Sara stood and fell into his arms.

Johnny gave the top of her wet head a kiss.

"Thank you, Johnny," she whispered.

"And you'll let me know your decision, right? No pulling me along just because you're afraid to tell me to go away."

"I promise, Johnny. You'll be the first to know."

He smiled again. "Yeah, I better be. Who else would put up with your Adam West fixation?"

"It's not so much a fixation as it is a hobby."

Johnny laughed. "Sara, you're not fooling anyone but yourself. You have a thing for that dude, and he's old enough to be your father."

"So now you're saying I have a father fixation?"

"No, you just have a thing for older men. It's a good thing I'm two years older than you, or I'd be out of the running."

They stepped out of the embrace, and smiled shyly at each other.

"You know, Johnny, I've figured out a few things about me and Mr. West. Want to hear them?"

Johnny reached for the knob on the kitchen door. "Let's save that conversation for another time, okay? I have to get to work. Some of us don't have the summers off like other lucky folks."

"Johnny?" Sara called as he stepped through the doorway. Johnny turned to look at her. "Thanks. I really mean it," she said.

"Sure, Gal Wonder." He shot a rueful grin in her direction and was gone.

CHAPTER NINETEEN

Sara lifted her eyes from the wine stain on her carpet and scanned the living room in search of the culprit. The party was in full swing, and her house was packed with friends and invited guests. She was fully occupied with making sure that everyone was comfortable, had a preferred drink in one hand and a tasty *hors d'oeuvres* in the other. True to her word, Gertie had made an array of cookies and pastries to satisfy anyone's sweet tooth. Dog was spending the evening at her mother's house, and Sara hated to think what havoc he was creating without supervision.

Sara knew that she should be interacting with her guests, especially the men, on a more personal level. She didn't want to disappoint her mother and sister by playing the wallflower at her own party, and yet she couldn't summon up enough interest or energy to play the captivating ingénue either. The earlier conversation with Johnny still ran through her mind.

"Do you want me to go away?" he had asked her.

She took a glance around her living room to see who she might want to speak with. There was no one special who captured her attention.

Still scanning the room, she gasped aloud and nearly spilled the glass of white Zinfandel in her hand. Either she was hallucinating, or she was seeing her college boyfriend, Sam Howard, standing next to her bookcase. It was impossible, and yet, there he was, in her home, scanning her collection of Heinlein books. When he looked her way, Sara could tell that he was trying to place her, as she had done with him. His blonde eyebrows were slightly furrowed, and his blue eyes narrowed. They were so far from their original place in time together, the University of Connecticut, that Sara knew it was possible he might not remember her. She had changed, of course, and despite all her attempts to hold on to her youth, she was treading on that slippery slope of middle age.

No doubt he thought he knew Sara, but wasn't sure from where, because this meeting was outside a familiar context. Like when you see your dentist at Wal-Mart and actually pass her by with a slight nod, before realizing exactly who she is.

Abruptly, Sara put her glass down and went to the kitchen. Seeing Sam was confusing her. He lived in Connecticut, last she knew. Why would he be in Pittsburgh, let alone here in her home?

And maybe he didn't *want* to reconnect with her. Maybe, if he did realize who she was, he would run for the door. Maybe he would think he wasn't welcome here.

Why was she so excited to see him, anyway? Sam had dumped her, thoroughly and without remorse. He had taken her college-girl heart and stamped his country-boy shoes all over it. When she had found him in his dorm room, naked between the sheets with another girl, it was the end of everything. A year of romance was ended by his need to sleep with the first girl who wiggled her fingers at him. Or whatever she had wiggled.

She saw him only once after she had caught him *in flagrante delicto*. He had come to her apartment in the middle of the night, months later, banging on her door, rip-roaring drunk and begging to be taken back. Sara had never even opened the door. She had told him to go away and turned off the lights. He had silently left, hopefully with his tail between his legs.

Now here he was, Sam Howard, in her home, looking even better with grey at his temples and small lines beside his mouth. He looked so familiar and yet so unknown at the same time. Sara had the urge to forgive him for his past transgressions. It would be nice to put a better ending to their story.

In the kitchen, from the highest cabinet over the sink, Sara pulled
down a bottle of liquor, hidden behind the oatmeal box. It was time for
the stronger stuff. She rinsed out the blender, which had been used to
make margaritas earlier in the evening, and measured the correct portions
of crème and alcohol. The blender whirred for a few moments, and then
Sara poured a luscious White Russian into a tall glass. She wanted to
chug it down, but knew that she had to be careful. Its sweetness belied its
strength. Perhaps she should take a lesson from this drink, she thought
to herself, as she held it up to the light to let the ice reflect. Her emotions
were strong, and she should try to engulf them all at once.

"Whatever you're looking for, I doubt you'll find it in that glass,"
a deep voice said from behind her.

She knew that voice. She forced her own to be steady.

"Oh, I don't know. I think oblivion can be found with enough White
Russians." She turned to face Sam. Her heart started racing. He had
matured into such a handsome man, how could she resist his charms?

"Are things so bad that you need to lose yourself in drink?"

"More that you might imagine. Or remember."

"Far be it from me to say that a drink doesn't fit the bill, now and
then." He took step closer to her. "And, Sara...I do remember many
things."

Dammit, she could feel his warm breath on her hair!

Sara slid past him and fussed with rinsing the blender in the
sink. "That's funny," she said. "That night in your college dorm, you
weren't having any trouble forgetting me."

She felt his hand on her shoulder.

"You have no idea how I've regretted what happened," he said.
"I've often wished I could take back that night. I am so sorry."

Sara continued washing the blender. Tears that couldn't be
stopped leaked out and down her cheek. She surreptitiously wiped
them on her sleeve while directing a harsh spray into the blender.
Suds flew up and hit her face. She laughed nervously.

"I don't know why seeing you is affecting me this way. I'm
jumpy...and I'm getting suds all over the place!" She slammed
the blender down on the counter, splashing more soapsuds on the
bodice of her dress. Indignant and embarrassed, she whirled around.

"So how the heck are you, Sam? It's been, what, twenty years, give or take a decade? Are you married? Have any kids? I didn't get too far in that department. I was married once—didn't work out. I live here alone with my goldfish, Goldie, and some mutt that I'm babysitting. I have great friends, my mom and my sister, of course..." Thoughts of Johnny lurked at the corners of her conscience. Was she betraying him? She pushed the thoughts aside as the alcohol began to soothe her. "So what's your story?"

Sam just stared at her for a few quiet moments. Was he ashamed of something, or just concocting a lie?

"I guess you could say that I'm in between wives at the moment. Things don't always work out the way you plan them, do they? "

Red alerts went off in her head. "Uh, yeah, sorry. That's true enough. I could be the poster child for marriages gone wrong. It's just that having you show up in my house after all these years has rattled me. Especially since the purpose of this party is to find me a new love interest."

"Are you serious?"

"I'm afraid so. This is a match-making party sponsored by my over-zealous friends and family. But let's put that aside for a moment. Sam, what in the hell are you doing here?"

Sam took a sip of his wine then smiled warily. "I came with Joe Norris. We work together, and—"

"Joe!" Sara whispered with narrowed eyes. "I might have known."

"Yeah, I was in town to work out a contract with Joe. He asked me if I wanted to come to a party with him. I didn't realize that I was going to be just another guy in your lineup."

"So you don't live around here?"

"Nope. I'm in Watertown, Connecticut, same as always."

"Then this is a whopper of a coincidence. You. Me. Here in my home."

"Things like this don't happen to me every day, that's for sure."

"Really? You've certainly had enough girlfriends to make a few random meetings a possibility." *And wives, too, apparently,* she thought to herself.

"Now hold on. There was one other girl during the year we were dating—"

"I figure if you did it to me, then you surely did it to others."

Sam stood away from the counter and put down his glass. "I guess I deserve that. And for a while, in college, I suppose it was true. I was young and sowing all the oats I could." He raised his eyebrows emphatically at her to make his point. "But I did change. Over time, I have changed."

Sara didn't believe him, not one bit. "Well, that's good. It's a good thing to change and... become a better person." She realized that she suddenly wanted to end this conversation. She was starting to see a pattern in her life—Johnny in high school, Sam in college, her ex-husband...She kept picking cheaters. Was that because of some flaw in her?

But Sam apparently did not want to send the conversation. "It's too bad that I met you early in my life, Sara. I'm sorry you were hurt by my selfish behavior."

"Water under the bridge," Sara tossed the phrase off lightly. She didn't really mean it, but it was the easiest thing to say at that moment.

Stop talking, Sam, please stop talking!

"I don't think so." Sam took a step towards her. "Those tears you just shed were not about nothing."

It was a lie. It was a line. Yet Sara felt herself trembling and hated herself for it.

"Don't come any closer," she warned as his toes met hers.

"I won't," Sam said softly. "I need to tell you again that I am very, very sorry, and that I regret my past mistake."

"So you're apologizing now, after all this time?"

"Yes. I never should have cheated on you. You were one of the best things in my life, and I lost you because of a stupid impulse. A momentary lapse. I hope you'll forgive me."

"I don't know. I guess so," she whispered. He did sound sincere, the scoundrel. And it would be nice to get some closure on the whole ugly incident.

"Then," Sam said, "Let's go somewhere, relax, and swap life stories."

Sara had to smile, "That sounds like a great idea, except I'm sort of the hostess of this party. I need to pay attention to my guests. You know, make sure their glasses are full and the bowls have plenty of chips."

Sam returned a regretful smile. "Okay. Not an ideal time. How about I call you tomorrow morning? I'm in Pittsburgh till Tuesday, so maybe we can have a nice dinner out tomorrow night."

She thought about Johnny. How would he feel if she went out with Sam? Then again, Sam was just an old friend. There was no law against having dinner with an old friend was there? After all, she didn't *have* to meet Sam for dinner if she didn't totally feel comfortable with it. She could just say no. And that made her say, "I guess we could do that."

She pulled out a pad of paper and a pen from a kitchen drawer and wrote down her phone number. "Here you go. Good seeing you again, Sam."

"Yeah. Pleasant surprise." Sam gave Sara a soft kiss on her cheek. "But I think, since you're busy, I'm gonna get out of here. I'll say goodbye to Joe and see myself out."

Sara watched after him, chugged down the last of her drink, then decided she had better rejoin the party, It wouldn't be long before one of the gals or her mother noticed that she was absent from the festivities.

Re-entering the living room, knowing that the gals would also take her to task if she didn't mingle, she approached a tall stranger who was not otherwise engaged. "Hi, I'm Sara."

The stranger flicked his eyes once to the left nervously then nodded his head. "Indeed," he said. "Well, good for you."

Sara was taken aback. "What?"

He gave her a direct look this time, with green penetrating eyes. "I mean, it's good to be you, isn't it? You're pretty and confident. And clearly you have lots of friends. So good for you. But it doesn't matter to me, really, since I'm leaving momentarily. As soon as I finish this beer, in fact." He waved the half-full bottle in front of her.

Sara stared. He was tall, built like a tree trunk, and incredibly rude. She sputtered a reply. "Gee, sorry you think the party stinks. Don't let me stop you from leaving. In fact, let me show you to the door." She may not have wanted to be at this train wreck of a party either, but this man's brutal frankness was too much.

"Hey. No offense intended," he said with an almost-smile. To his credit, he did have a nice smile.

"Sorry, but offense taken," she said sharply. "This happens to be my house and my party."

After taking a large gulp from the beer bottle, the stranger nodded his head again. "Yes, of course it is."

"What's that supposed to mean?"

"You pretty girls always have these parties where there are more men than women. That's so you can have the guys falling all over themselves for your attention." He sighed loudly. "I don't play those games."

"Who the hell are you? And who invited you anyway? You're obnoxious. You're... tall. You're—you're a *dork!*"

As lame as her stumbling diatribe was, she thought at least it would offend him. Instead, he laughed. "You're very perceptive. Got it in three. I am tall, obnoxious and, sadly, a dork." He wiped his hand on his jeans then extended his arm towards Sara. "I'm Alex, Mitchell's friend. I was dragged to this party with the promise of good alcohol and bad women."

Sara just stared at his hand, and he eventually returned it to his side. Looking down at his nearly empty beer bottle, he said, "The alcohol is okay, but there isn't a loose woman on the premises." He scanned the room, then turned back to look at Sara. "Unless?" He raised his eyebrows with insinuation heavy in his dark eyes.

She stared back, uncertain what to say. What was *wrong* with this man? This was beyond "Socially awkward," this was—wait, did he just call her a loose woman? Suddenly she knew exactly what to say.

"Get the hell out of here."

She said it quietly, calmly, but, she hoped, dangerously.

Alex put his empty bottle on the shelf of her bookcase, and zipped up his sweatshirt. "Too bad," he said with almost no intonation. "Just when things were getting interesting. I have a suspicion, Sara, that you probably find this party as dull as I do."

"What?" she demanded. Okay, she'd just ordered him out, but he was so—so *weird,* so outside-the-box, that he presented a puzzle to be solved. Sara had a hard time resisting puzzles.

"I was watching you talk to that blonde guy in the kitchen, and I could tell you just wanted him to go away. Like you want me to go away. Yeah, but he's definitely not your type. Even though there was some electricity, he's not what you need."

"'Electricity?' What in the world is—what makes you think I wanted him to—You don't even know me! How can you stand there and say who is or isn't my type?"

He shrugged. "Maybe I'm wrong, but, from where I'm standing, I doubt that the other guy would know what to make of you."

"Oh, really?"

"I mean, okay, you're easy on the eyes—"

"*Thank* you," she said testily.

"Not every man can handle a woman who has curves that never quit—"

"I *get* it."

"But you're not just another pretty face."

This caught her completely off guard, and caused her to soften her tone just a little. "Go on."

"You're quirky." He looked around. "You have Michael Whelan prints on the walls and a Spock action figure by the TV. And the replica Batmobile over on that shelf? In a display case, like it's a prize possession?"

"So?"

"So. Quirky. That's a hard sell, and I bet that guy wouldn't end up buying. Plus, you have a fiery temper. Who knows, maybe that fire equates to passion in the bedroom?" He stepped closer to her. "That guy in the kitchen was a straight arrow. You'd be bored of him within a week. And the other guys at this party? No one here could match your fire. You need someone who wants you for who you are, and not who they want you to be."

He began to turn towards the front door, but Sara grabbed his sleeve. "I suppose you think you're the one who could light my fire?"

"Probably. But taking you on would be … complicated. It would mean more than a roll in the hay. I can't do that; I'm just not wired that way. So thanks for the beer… Sara."

He threaded his way through the party guests and was gone.

She'd had two interactions with men at this party, one a wild surprise and the other a weird disturbance. Weary of the party, she wanted nothing more than to escape to her bedroom.

"Who was that?" Nicole was at her elbow.

"I don't know. Some friend of Mitchell's. But he wasn't my Prince Charming."

"Excuse me?"

"You set up this party so that I could meet the man of my dreams, right? Well, instead it looks like I've just met a toad."

"So? Doesn't a kiss turn a frog into a prince?"

"A frog, yes. I don't think fairy tales ever mentioned toads. Anyway, this," Sara swept her arm to indicate the predominantly-male crowd, "is more of a nightmare than a fairy tale. Did you know that Sam was here, my college sweetheart?"

"Seriously? The one you caught—?"

"Yep. It's like some warped version of *This is Your Life.*"

"I'm sorry, Sara. I had really hoped you'd get to relax and enjoy yourself tonight."

"I've never liked being the center of attention. That's your thing, not mine." Indeed, Sara thought, the shine in Nicole's eyes said that she *was* enjoying the attention of all these men. Why couldn't Sara simply relax and enjoy it that way?

"I think I've had enough partying for one night," Sara said with a yawn.

"Hey, wait—Did that guy from down the street show up, the one with the cute kid?"

"David? God no! Didn't you see today's paper? He's probably taking out a restraining order."

"I'm not sure what to do with you, Sara."

"Then, for once, just let me be. Please?" Sara met Nicole's eyes directly. "I need to figure out things on my own. I agreed to this party, but I really didn't think it through. If anything, this party has caused more problems than it solved. And no," she added before Nicky even opened her mouth, "I don't want to get into them right now. I know you and Mom love me, and I'm grateful. Now, in the interest of my sanity, get these people out of my house!"

CHAPTER TWENTY

Sara ran a brush lightly through her hair then flicked off the light in the bathroom. She was as ready as she would ever be for this date with Sam. He had called her that morning while she'd been bustling around her apartment, cleaning up stray napkins and empty drink cups from behind the couch and under the coffee table. The remains of the party were thankfully few due to the thoughtfulness of her mother and sister the evening before. Sara had retired to bed before the party ended, locking her bedroom door and wearing sound-proof ear plugs.

Sara hadn't wanted to appear anti-social; she just wanted to be unavailable. She had survived most of the evening fairly well, especially when she focused on party things like food and music. But when she actually had to interact with the opposite sex, she had found herself in a strange state, acutely aware of her own words echoing in her ears. It was disconcerting, especially when she realized how false she sounded. She had tried to put her best foot forward with her potential suitors—admittedly to please her meddling family and girlfriends—but the truth was that she had no interest in any of them.

However, reconnecting with Sam had been somewhat of a jolt. While she still held reservations about his character, she was willing to set her doubts aside and give him a second chance… as a friend.

When he had called that morning, she had felt a flutter of excitement about seeing him again. Sam said he would pick her up and drive downtown for dinner. His restaurant choice had been somewhat offbeat: the buffet at the Rivers Casino. Sara wasn't into the gambling scene. She had been hoping for a more sedate and out-of-the-way restaurant that would have been better suited to an evening of conversation. But Sam was from out of town. Maybe he just wasn't familiar with the diversity of dining choices Pittsburgh had to offer. Sara decided to go with the flow.

Sara wore a little black dress with patterned straps at the neckline that showed a peek of cleavage. With matching black leather bag and heels, she felt comfortably chic. She rarely had a chance to dress up for work, so this was a refreshing opportunity to step out of the norm.

If only the Caped Crusader could see me now! Sara thought. *There's a new Catwoman in town.*

The doorbell rang, and Sara moved quickly to answer it.

"Sam." She smiled brightly at the handsome man in the dark suit and red silk tie as he stood in the doorway. "My, you do clean up nicely."

"As do you," Sam replied. "Last night you were lovely, but tonight you are spectacular."

Sara laughed, "Always a sweet talker." She ran to her kitchen table and grabbed her purse. "I'm looking forward to this," she said, rather breathlessly. "It's been a while since I've been somewhere other than the local ice cream shop."

"I'm glad you are, though I have to admit I've been nervous ever since I called you this morning. It's been a long time. A lot of things have changed with me, so I'm sure it's the same with you."

"But even after all these years, I'll bet we find some things in common. Just like we did in college."

"You mean besides the obvious?" Sam asked.

"You were more to me than just a lover to me, Sam. But now, I'd be happy if we could be friends."

Sam raised his eyebrows but remained silent as they walked out into the early evening sunshine. A mid-sized blue Chevy sat at the curb in front of the building.

"I apologize for our transportation for the evening. I'm more of a sports car kind of guy myself, but the rental agency only had this. I guess it will have to do for now."

"It's fine," Sara said. "What do you drive at home?"

"A Mazda Miata. She's a sweet thing on the roads."

Sara remembered calling Johnny's new car a "beaut," and how he had preened at the compliment, even though she had been teasing him. She thought that if men were as free with their compliments to women as they were with their cars, relations between the sexes might improve markedly.

After buckling in, Sara took a moment to observe Sam more closely. The years had been good to him, even with the wrinkles around the eyes and the blond hair fading to grey. He was still a striking man with deep blue eyes and the athletic build of a younger man. He was fortunate; he still had that indefinable allure that could turn the heads of women of all ages. Sara felt pleased to be sitting next to him and wondered if this new friendship would continue on after this evening. Sam would be going back to Connecticut, but that didn't mean they couldn't have a long distance friendship if all went well between them.

"I'm curious about your restaurant choice for tonight. Why the dinner buffet at the casino?" Sara asked.

Sam turned his head a little too quickly. "What? Isn't it good enough?"

"No, no!" said Sara, hoping she hadn't touched a nerve. "I just was asking because it's not something most people would think of doing. It's fine, really." She rested her hand on his upper arm to reassure him, but what she really wanted was some reassurance herself. They had only begun the evening, and it seemed that she had stepped on some sore spot. "I'm looking forward to the buffet. I hear that the crab legs are delicious."

Sam seemed calm, but he remained silent.

"You okay, Sam?" she asked gently.

"Yeah. Sure. Sorry about that. I get a little sensitive to questions about the things I do. It's probably a holdover from my marriages. The wives never seemed to want to do what I wanted to do, and they were always jumping on me." He sighed deeply.

"Geez. Sorry I reminded you of unpleasant times. I promise it was an innocent question, Sam."

"Okay." He glanced over at Sara and said, "How could I let a gorgeous woman like you get me down?"

Sara was confused by his statement. It sounded a bit backhanded, admitting that she had in fact, gotten him down. Surely he had twisted up what he wanted to say. Sara decided it was best to leave it alone.

They parked in the casino's covered garage and rode the elevator to the main casino floor. As the doors opened, they were assaulted by loud music, ringing bells, shouts, and laughter. A haze of tobacco smoke floated over the room of slot machines and gaming tables. The casino was alive with flashing lights and crowds of people of all ages and nationalities.

Sara clung to Sam's arm, bewildered by the attack on her senses. She had never been to this casino. Gertie was a gambler to the core and rode the senior citizen bus down to the casino weekly with her pals. Sara never chastised her mother for risking her money. Her father had left Gertie with a healthy portfolio, and Gertie's gambling was modest. She also knew that Gertie would have chewed her head off had Sara attempted to stand in the way of her gambling. Sara had gone with Gertie to a casino in West Virginia a few years back where it had been relatively quiet and filled with an older crowd during the daytime. It had been nothing like this.

"Where's the buffet restaurant?" Sara shouted, hoping to be heard above the din.

When Sam didn't answer, Sara looked up to find Sam's eyes bright and shining with excitement. He scanned the casino floor, mesmerized by the incessant activity and sounds.

"Sam?" Sara shouted again.

"Okay, yeah," Sam said, clearly not hearing Sara at all.

"Sam!" Sara tried again, this time pulling at his arm. He looked down at Sara as if she were a stranger. He shook his head, and ran his hand absentmindedly through his hair.

"Dinner. Restaurant. Right." He pulled Sara's hand off his arm and intertwined his fingers between hers. "Okay, let's find that buffet."

Sara pulled in a calming breath then pointed to an overhead sign. "Thataway," she said.

They entered the restaurant after Sam prepaid for their meals. The restaurant was brightly lit and reminded Sara of an upscale cafeteria. They were seated by a window overlooking the Mon River, so they would be able to watch the tugboats pushing barges of coal upriver as the sun set. After a few moments lost in the view, Sara turned to ask Sam what he thought.

He had already left the table and gone to the bar.

Wasn't it customary, when a gentleman—or anyone, for that matter—went to the bar, for them to ask their dinner date if they wanted something? A chilling thought hit her: maybe Sam expected her to buy her own drink, since alcohol was not included with the buffet? No, that was silly. He wouldn't—

Sam turned from the bar with only one drink glass in his hand.

"Hey! This is pretty nice, huh?" He smiled at Sara as he took a long drink then placed the glass on the table. "Let's get to it. That pile of crab legs is calling my name."

Sara followed Sam to the stack of clean plates, but lost him soon after as he forged on ahead to the seafood table. Sara sighed and walked through the serving areas until she found the salad fixings. She also added some fresh turkey slices and a bit of cheese tortellini to her plate. When she returned to the table, she saw that Sam had left his plate of crab legs and once again had gone to the bar. Something quivered in the pit of Sara's stomaach. Sam seemed too energized, too turned on by the casino. She took a bit of salad, not tasting much of anything.

"Hey, babe!" Sam said—okay, slurred—as he returned to the table, a second drink in hand. "This place is fabulous. Much better than some of the casinos we have in Connecticut."

"Oh? Do you go often?"

"Whenever I get a chance." Sam cracked open a crab leg and sucked the tender meat from its shell.

Crab juice and butter ran down his chin and onto his plate. Sara was tempted to take a napkin and wipe his face, but Sam was already shredding his next crab leg. Sara hoped that the crab meat in his stomach would neutralize his levels of alcohol. But after two drinks in five minutes, it seemed a poor bet.

Sara picked at her meal, realizing that she was the designated driver whether she wanted to be or not. This was not the evening she had envisioned with Sam.

"Did I tell you that you look beautiful tonight?" Sam asked in between sips of his drink. "You haven't changed a bit. I tell you, I knew how to pick 'em back in the day." He banged his glass down on the table. "Now, not so much."

Sara gave him a faint smile. "Do tell."

Sam stopped eating, and looked at Sara sideways. "You making fun of me?"

Sara felt an instant's panic. Did Sam have anger issues as well as problems with drinking? In a calm, even tone that belied her worries, she said, "Nope. I really want to know. What were the Howard wives like?"

"I'll tell you," he said waving his almost empty glass in the air. "My wives have been greedy, controlling harpies. My first wife never stopped complaining about stuff around the house, like how I didn't mow the lawn or take out the garbage. But Tracey, wife number, uh, three, I think, she says I'm a loser and that I waste all my money on the horses and at the casinos. What does she know? I am *this* close." Sam held his thumb and his pointer finger an inch apart. "This close to a major win. I can feel it."

Sara nodded as if she was impressed with his grandiose claim, but she was actually busy processing what she thought she had just heard. Sam had spoken of his first wife in the past tense, but talked about this Tracey in the present, as if she was a part of his life in the here and now. Was Sam currently married?

"So, Sam, um, does Tracey know you're out with me tonight?" Sara asked casually.

He laughed idiotically. "Hell, no! That witch doesn't need to know nothin' about what I do when I'm out of town." He turned in his chair and stood up. "I'm getting one more drink. Then let's say we try our hand at the blackjack tables? I'm feeling lucky tonight!"

Sara could barely contain her fury. And Sam...the idiot just didn't get it. He didn't even feel ashamed that he was out on a date, cheating on his wife, with the girl he'd cheated on in college.

One of the girls he had cheated on in college.

Carefully Sara eased her cell phone out of her purse and pushed the speed dial button.

"Joe?" she whispered, her hand covering the phone as she glanced furtively back at Sam by the bar. "Could you come and get me? I'm at the Rivers Casino on a dinner date with your old pal, Sam. He's had way too much to drink. Did you know he's married? He also gets angry and scares me."

Joe called out, "On my way!" That's what Batman used to say to Commissioner Gordon when he was called to rescue the city from another nefarious villain. She could count on Joe to help her.

Sam led Sara to the betting tables after dinner. She stood behind him as he lost hand after hand of blackjack. He seemed to be too drunk to follow the game play and accused the dealer of tampering with the deck. Sam continued to knock back drinks—drinks which were complimentary on the casino floor.

Sara heaved a sigh of relief when her cell phone vibrated in her purse. She told Joe where she was, not caring if Sam overheard her conversation. It probably didn't matter. Sam was too far gone to even notice that she was there.

"Joe!" she called when her dear friend came into view. Then she actually squeaked when she saw who was on his heels.

"Johnny? What are you doing here?"

"Sorry, Sara," Joe interrupted. "But I didn't know where the casino was. Johnny and I were hanging out when you called. So since I've never been here, he offered to drive me down."

Johnny stood silently behind Joe, watching Sara, seeming oblivious to the flashing lights and ringing bells of the slot machines all around them.

"Sara," Johnny said, nodding once.

Sara felt a tremor of anxiety run through her. She knew how this looked to Johnny, but she couldn't find the words to explain the situation. So instead, she turned back to Joe, and said,"I'm just glad you made it. I want to get out of here...now."

Sara, Johnny and Joe all turned as one to watch as Sam wobbled side to side on his stool at the betting table.

Joe went over to Sam, slipped his arms around Sam's shoulders and said, "Okay, big guy. Time to go home."

Sam looked confused as he recognized Joe. "Whatcha doin' here, buddy?"

"I'm here to take you home," Joe replied firmly. "Play time is over."

Sam lifted his chin and defiantly squared his shoulders, but Joe and Johnny joined forces to deftly pull Sam from his stool. Together the men marched him towards the casino's elevators. Sam was too far gone to even lodge a protest.

"Sara, you can ride home with Johnny in his car. I'll take this drunken-ass dude to his hotel after you show me where you parked and after you dig in his pockets for the car keys."

Sara rolled her eyes. "The keys are in the pocket of his suit jacket. No need for fishing around."

"Good," Joe replied, while breathing heavily from supporting Sam. The elevator door opened and they all stepped inside. Sara pushed the floor number and the elevator began to rise.

"Sara, I'm so sorry about this. He really did seem like a nice guy when I was working with him. I didn't know you were going to go out with him, or I would have checked his credentials ahead of time."

The elevator dinged, and the doors opened to the parking garage.

"Joe, let's keep walking," Johnny said loudly. "This guy is going to be too heavy to carry if he passes out." As if to prove Johnny's point, Sam lolled his head to one side and moaned.

Johnny's voice was tight, and his eyes focused on the pavement ahead. He hadn't looked at Sara once.

Sara led them to the parked sedan.

Joe grabbed the keys from Sam's jacket and unlocked the car doors while Johnny supported Sam up against the side of the car. Together Johnny and Joe managed to push and maneuver Sam into the back seat, where he collapsed in a heap.

Joe asked Sara, "That's it, then. Are you okay?"

"Yes. I'm fine. Be careful driving back. I can't thank you enough for coming to my rescue." She hugged him quickly. "And don't worry. None of this is your fault."

As Joe pulled away and head down the ramp to the casino exit, Johnny took Sara's elbow and guided her to a safer distance. "My car's this way. Come on." He walked briskly away from Sara and across the garage floor. She struggled to keep up with Johnny's pace, but she didn't dare say a word. She knew he was angry.

Johnny unlocked the doors automatically and slipped into the driver's seat without offering to close Sara's door. He had never failed to close her door before. They sat in dark silence for several moments.

"Johnny, it's not what it looks like."

"Don't, Sara. Just don't." He turned the key in the ignition and started the car. "I can stand almost anything from you, except lies."

"Johnny. You don't understand. It wasn't a date. Well, it was a dinner date, but it wasn't a date-date."

Johnny drove down the ramp and out into the spring evening. City lights illuminated the building and bridges in soft golds and silvers. Johnny remained silent, his eyes on the road.

"Sam was an old boyfriend. From college. We were just catching up. It's been a long time, and I thought we could be friends. Just friends. I didn't know that he was a gambler and a drinker. I didn't know."

"And if he hadn't been? Would it have been a 'date-date,' Sara? Would you have maybe started up something again?" Johnny's voice was bitter and cutting.

"No! That's not what I'm saying! I thought we could be friends..." Her voice tapered off. She seemed to be losing a war with this battle. Nothing she said seemed to make a difference to Johnny.

"Sara, didn't I tell you yesterday that I couldn't handle it if you started going out with other guys? It was just yesterday! You couldn't even wait a week."

"It wasn't a date," Sara said, breaking into tears. She couldn't fight anymore when she didn't even know what side she wanted to be on. It felt like she should be with Johnny, but his assumptions, his jealousy, made her want to scream. This is how men acted, totally, insufferably sure of themselves, even while they were hurting you. Sara began to sob in earnest. She felt destroyed.

Johnny stole a glance at her then sighed heavily. "I'm sorry, Sara. I didn't mean to attack you. I just couldn't stand seeing you with that jerk. It killed me."

Sara glared at him through her tears. "You didn't want to believe me. You didn't trust me! How dare you assume anything about me? How dare you?!"

Johnny drove through empty suburban streets. Some people were gathered inside a pizzeria; others were leaving a movie theater. Everything seemed far removed from the tension that hummed inside the car. Sara continued to savagely swipe at the tears on her cheeks. Johnny seemed lost in his thoughts. And then when he spoke the words were devoid of emotion.

"You're right," Johnny said. "I'm a complete ass. I won't bother you again, Sara." He turned and briefly met her eyes. "I'm sorry."

Sara sat like an unmovable, impenetrable stone. She couldn't feel anything, nor did she want to. She only wanted to be home and away from all the drama and pain. She would be fine if she could just get under the covers and hide from the world. She would be fine if she never saw Johnny again. Only why did it hurt so badly to think that this was the end of their story?

Johnny pulled up in front of her house. The front porch light shone like a beacon of comfort. She pushed her car door open and slowly got out of the car. As she walked away from the car—from Johnny and, from any hope of a future relationship—she wondered where everything had gone wrong. But it didn't really matter. She was home. She heard Johnny slam her door closed then turn the wheel on the gravel as he steered away from her house. She entered her house, throwing her keys on a side table in the living room.

"Dog?" she called into the unnatural quiet of her home. She walked into the kitchen, through the living room and into her bedroom. Dog wasn't anywhere to be found. Sara racked her brain—had she taken him to Gertie's? After the party, the cleanup and tonight's disasters, she felt foggy and uncertain. Maybe she'd left Dog outside in the yard. She did that sometimes, now that the weather was nice. Dog really enjoyed being outdoors. All she had to do was leave some fresh water in a bowl. He rarely barked, and he could chase all the butterflies and crickets to his heart's content. Yes, she was pretty sure that's what she had done.

She stepped through her kitchen door and peered around her yard, lit only with a small outdoor light. The cicadas were chirping fiercely, and a warm breeze wafted by. There was the stake in the ground, a half-empty water bowl, but nothing else. "Arf?" she called plaintively.

CHAPTER TWENTY-ONE

Sara raced to her front door, throwing it open and tearing into the front yard. "Arf?" she called. She ran out into the empty street and looked in both directions. All was quiet; nothing moved except the fresh leaves on the budding trees. She ran down the middle of the street, panic rising in her. "Arf!" she yelled. One house turned on its porch light, and Sara felt like an intruder in her own neighborhood. She stopped at the street corner and looked in all directions. She heard the buzz of the street light above her. There was no sign of life no matter where she turned, and Sara realized the futility of searching in the dark.

If Arf wasn't close to the house, then that meant he could be anywhere. She'd been gone for several hours, and a dog could get far away in that amount of time. She'd just have to wait until morning to begin a proper search. She slowly returned to her house. Taking one last all-encompassing look, she noticed that her mailbox was stuffed with envelopes and circulars. She grabbed the mail, went inside and locked her front door.

Sara walked to the kitchen, where she tossed the mail onto the table. She kicked off her heels, then reached into her cabinet for her tea tin while grabbing a mug from the dish rack. She microwaved water, dropped in an Earl Grey teabag, and sagged into a chair, exhaustion washing over her. Everything she'd just experienced felt like a heavy weight on her shoulders and in her heart. By now she would have expected to have just gone numb, but she felt the wetness of tears on her cheeks.

Sara had never seen herself as introspective, someone who spent time analyzing her own thoughts and actions; but she needed to understand why she had spent so much time being so *sad*. It wasn't enough anymore to cruise through life, hoping that everything would work out for the best. Fate had brought her to this point, and Fate hadn't done a very good job. *She* needed to step up and choose where she would go from here.

She tried to figure out exactly when the trouble had started, but all she could think about was tonight's catastrophe. The dinner with Sam had been utterly ridiculous, an excuse for him to wallow in his addictions. She was grateful for Joe's help (and Johnny's, she realized painfully). She only wished that she had called Joe earlier in the evening. Hell, she wished that she had never gone with Sam to begin with.

She had a habit of giving people second and third chances to alter poor behavior, but she knew that had to stop. She had to respect herself and make a stand for her own happiness. Someone like Sam had no place in her life.

And Johnny? She hadn't expected him to show up with Joe, to see her with Sam. Was it guilt she felt, because she had seen another man socially? Or was it just humiliation that *anyone* had seen her with a scumbag like Sam? Well, except Joe, of course. Joe kept all her secrets, just as Jen or Char would have. Joe was an amazing gay best friend—who was, it turned out, mysteriously not gay.

So why was she humiliated that Johnny, or someone not on her secret-keepers list, would see her with Sam? Because she didn't want people to think less of her.

Dammit, she especially didn't want *Johnny* to think less of her. If only he'd given her a chance to explain.

But he hadn't. He'd tried her, convicted her and sentenced her in his own mind, sentenced her to not having her side of the story heard. And so she had had to defend herself. It had been so hard to stand up and challenge him. He was her friend—at least!—but her honor was at stake. No one, not even Johnny Nash, would be allowed to question her integrity.

Oh, Johnny had apologized. That was something. But it was too soon to think about reconciliation. Their friendship might actually be over, once and for all. Johnny had left her tonight without a word or a backward glance. And she had done the same to him.

Did she actually want to be with Johnny? He had shown a bitter, jealous side that had raised all sorts of red flags. Her ex-husband had been a control freak, to the Nth degree. She would not tolerate being controlled by anyone, not by Johnny, not by any man. She had waited so long to see if Johnny was the one man who could give her what she needed to be happy in a relationship. Tonight's jealousy may have been the sign she needed to make her decision.

But that was not an issue anymore, was it? Johnny had effectively said good-bye. Problem solved.

Sara removed the tea bag from her almost-forgotten mug and set it on a napkin. She sipped. It was still warm enough. The soothing taste calmed her, and she shuddered in a deep breath.

She couldn't believe that Dog—Arf—was gone. She had taken such good care of him, even though he'd been a responsibility that she'd rather not have to deal with. For heaven's sake, she even let him up on the sofa now when she was watching television. She couldn't imagine what she would say to Char if Arf didn't return. She had let her friend down, and she took that seriously.

She would call Animal Control in the morning. Maybe she could get together some of her friends for a search party. She'd send messages to Joe and Jen, and her mother and sister as well. But she wouldn't notify Char and Mitchell. She wouldn't tell them anything unless she was certain Arf was gone for good. She'd have to swear the others to secrecy until such a time as the bad news had to be delivered. Sara's tears started up again, and one even plopped into her cup of tea. She took a napkin from the holder and wiped her tears. She idly leafed through her mail, a distraction from the turmoil in her heart and head.

There was the cable bill, the auto insurance bill, some catalogs to throw out, along with grocery store circulars. Then there was an official-looking envelope. The return address was Los Angeles, California.

Who did she know in Los Angeles? Nobody. It must be—Sara's heart skipped a beat.

It could be from Adam West.

He was in California, or at least his agent was. She had sent her letters to a similar address. Slowly, she tore open the top of the envelope so that she wouldn't ruin the hand-written address or the postmark from LA.

Slipping the letter out, she brought it close to her heart for a few seconds to prolong the suspense. Maybe, just maybe, one good thing was going to come out of this day. Had Adam West really answered one of her letters? It would mean so much to have a personal response. She would have some tangible proof that she had made a connection with Adam West.

As she unfolded the letter, her heart sank. It was a form letter, signed only by some agency representative.

> *Dear Adam West Fan,*
>
> *While Mr. West appreciates mail from his loyal viewers, his work schedule does not permit him to send a reply to each and every item of correspondence he receives. He is grateful for your continued support and wishes you well in your future endeavors.*

The unknown signature was followed by a repeat of the L.A. address from the envelope. Sara carelessly let the letter slip onto her lap. As it drifted over the edge of her chair, she made a grab for it. That's when she saw the handwritten words in blue ink on the back of the paper. The handwriting was swooping, but easily deciphered.

It said, "You're not a superhero. Live the life you've been given."

Sara gasped and stood up. She read then reread the short message. *You're not a superhero.* She said the words aloud. "Live the life you've been given." It had to be from Adam West. It was in his handwriting. She could easily compare it to his signature on the convention photo.

She bit her lip. She hadn't really expected a reply from Adam West, but here it was. It wasn't a long formal letter with words of wisdom from her cherished hero. But somehow this hand-written note was more meaningful, despite its brevity.

Sara could easily read the intent of the message. She had asked Adam if she should become like Batman, alone and dedicated to her work. Adam was saying that she wasn't some superhero; she was a human, flesh and blood, with all the needs and desires of any other human. She wasn't meant to pull away from others, to build walls to keep herself safe from the hurt and pain that could happen.

It was true. She wasn't a Gal Wonder, no matter what Joe called her. She was Sara Goode, middle-aged, filled with faults and capable of making big mistakes. But she was also a good teacher, daughter, sister, friend—she was a good *person*. And maybe, someday, she could be someone who accepted the love of a good man, and loved him in return. Someone like Johnny, who made mistakes and had faults just as crazy as her own. Adam's letter had given her strength. She would make it through this day, and the next and the next. She would start living the life she had been given.

CHAPTER TWENTY-TWO

"Okay, troops. Listen up. We work in groups of two, with each person covering one side of their assigned street." Jen was in full glory as she gave the orders to the volunteers who would be searching for Arf. "Be sure to look in back yards, around playground equipment and any surrounding wooded areas. We can't rule out that Arf hasn't fallen into any ditches, drains or excavations. Here are pictures of the missing dog." Jen began handing out sheaths of paper covered in pictures of Arf and giving the contact information for when and if he was found.

"But, Jen, we all know what Arf looks like. We don't need these flyers," Gertie said, as she juggled with her handbag, a Starbucks coffee and a few flyers.

"The flyers are for giving out to folks in the area. The more eyes on the ground, the better success this operation will have." Jen said, making eye contact with Joe. He'd no doubt assisted her in the strategic planning for this search. He gave her a thumbs-up whenever she looked his way. "Flyers can also be posted on poles with thumbtacks." Jen held up a small bag of tacks. "Or the papers can be taped up." She raised her other hand to show a tape dispenser, as if anyone here might have trouble telling one from the other. It was the kind of thing Sara would need to do for her students, and perhaps Jen had to do for Principal Johnson.

"Give me one of each, then let's get this posse on the road," Gertie said. "There's a bingo down at the fire hall this afternoon, and I will be there when it starts." She pushed through those in front of her and grabbed a tack bag and a tape dispenser.

Sara rolled her eyes at her mother's impatience. It was too early in the morning to be dealing with Gertie's own brand of feisty. She knew she should be grateful that any of them had offered their time and assistance to search for Arf. But she was so tired. Her sleep had been fitful, with frequent trips outside to see if Arf might have wandered back home.

Sara had called Animal Control first thing that morning, but they hadn't picked up any dogs matching Arf's description. Sara had kept adding details as she talked to the representative, hoping that just one more piece of information would identify Arf . "He's golden with a few white splotches. Um, he has pointy ears when he's listening. He's not very big, probably less than medium-sized. And he swishes his tail really fast side to side when he's happy."

Sara wanted desperately to hear, "Yes! Your dog is right here, safe and sound." But that hadn't happened, and now Sara felt overwhelmed and scared. She just wanted Arf back home, where he belonged.

"Come on, Mom," Nicole called to Gertie. "I'll be your teammate. Hey, guys, we're off to do Spring Street." She took her mother by the elbow and escorted Gertie to the front door. "Mom, leave your purse here. There's nothing you need in there for a dog hunt."

"Oh, really, Ms. Smarty-Pants?" Gertie said. She reached inside her purse and pulled out a small bag of dog treats. "How about them apples?" she said triumphantly.

Nicky sighed, and said, "Okay. You win. Now let's go." They left Sara's house, arm in arm.

Sara surveyed the remaining volunteers. Jen and Joe would team up, as would the Mataluski sisters and several second grade teachers from May View Elementary. That left her to travel on foot...alone.

"If anyone spots Arf, please call my cell immediately." Sara said a silent prayer that Arf would be found soon. The scruffy mutt was probably tired and hungry.

Everyone eventually left her house, heading towards the neighborhood streets assigned to them by Jen. Sara had decided to stay in the immediate area, in case Arf showed up unexpectedly. She grabbed her house keys and reached the front door before she realized someone was standing on her front steps. "Did you forget some...?" Her question remained unfinished as she immediately recognized Johnny's profile.

Sara stood staring, mute at his unexpected presence. "Um, we're all looking for Arf." She cleared her throat. "He was gone, last night, when I got home. Animal Control doesn't have him, so it's up to us to find him."

Johnny nodded. "Yes, Joe texted me just a little while ago. He thought I might like to help with the search. Would you like my help, Sara?"

Sara swallowed hard. "That would be good, I guess. I mean, Joe didn't know that we aren't speaking." She gave a rueful smile. "Well, I guess we are technically speaking, but I mean..."

"I know what you mean, Sara. Don't sweat it," Johnny spoke gently, with a slight smile. "Where should we start looking?" He looked down the street to the right. "That way?"

"Yeah, sure." Sara locked her front door and joined Johnny as he strode up the sidewalk. At least today he was allowing her to match his pace, instead of the way he had practically run from her in the casino parking garage last evening.

They walked in silence, their eyes sweeping across lawns and gardens in the slowly awakening morning. Every now and then, Sara would tack a flyer to a phone pole.

"So, how did he get away?" Johnny asked, after handing a flyer to an elderly gentleman who was watering his vegetable patch.

"I'm not sure. I tied his leash to the post in the yard like I always do, but he must have gotten loose somehow. There was no leash there when I checked last night. The door to the fence was closed, and I couldn't find any holes under the fence where he could have escaped. But that doesn't mean he didn't find a way out. Obviously."

"Hmm... I hate to bring this up, but do you think it's possible that someone stole Arf?"

Sara stopped walking. "Stole him? But, he's a mutt! Who would want a scruffy old mutt?"

Johnny raised his hands in surrender. "It's just a thought, Sara. I'm not saying that's what happened. But based on what you just told me, Arf didn't escape."

"If someone took him, and I find them, they will live to regret it."

Johnny raised his eyebrows. "I see. So you'll transform a case of dog theft into murder one?"

"Not murder. I said they'd live." Sara began walking again, quickening her pace. "But they may wish they hadn't."

If Johnny had further thoughts on the subject, he kept them to himself. Sara was well aware that she wasn't open to anyone trying to reason with her right now.

As they rounded a street corner, they found a trim, white-haired gentleman holding one of Arf's flyers. "Mr. Johnson!" Sara exclaimed. "What are you doing here?"

"Oh, why hello, Sara," the Principal said, his eyes darting about with unease. No doubt he was embarrassed now to be seen by his staff. "I, ah, live a few streets away. Someone handed me this missing dog flyer. Thought I'd take a look." He gave a self-deprecating chuckle. "Guess I've sort of been at loose ends the past few days. Seemed like something useful to do."

"Mr. Johnson, that's my dog, Arf. Thank you so much for helping us out. Oh, and this is—" She stumbled. How to introduce this man who was, as usual, at her side when things went wrong? She settled on, "A *friend*, Johnny Nash."

While he shook Johnny's hand, the Principal said, "Well, Sara, I'm glad to be able to help you. I feel like I owe you a favor. After all, you sent Joe Norris over to help solve our little..." Again he looked embarrassed, "*mystery.*"

"Oh," said Sara. It had completely slipped her mind that she had been the one to recommend Joe. "I hope he was helpful."

"Helpful? I'll say. He's given me a new perspective on that whole situation. I've decided to stay on at the school and use this experience as an instructional tool for the students and the staff. I rescinded my resignation to the board yesterday."

She took his hand, felt tears coming to her eyes. "That's great news! You're making a lot of teachers—and students—very happy, whether they know it or not."

She was too happy right now to wonder if Joe had presented her idea as his own. She was just grateful that Mr. Johnson had listened.

"Well," Mr. Johnson said with renewed vigor, "let's see if we can't make you even happier by finding that dog of yours."

They traded their good-byes and continued on their search. Johnny checked an electric company work area that was cordoned off on the street. Sara walked ahead slowly, giving Johnny time to catch up with her.

"I recognize this street," she said. She stopped and looked around, squinting. "I've been here before." She took a few steps forward and then gasped when she recognized one of the houses on the street. "Oh my god, this is Bluebell Lane. That's Bobby Moore's house!"

"You mean the House of the Mad Shepherds?"

"I guess they weren't mad, just over-zealous." In her concern over Arf, her goodwill toward all dogs seemed to have increased. She hated the thought of little Arf being hurt. Mean as they were, she hated the thought of "The Girls" being harmed in any way either.

"'Over-zealous' is not what I heard."

"I swear that I'm going to permanently duct-tape Joe's mouth."

"Well, to be fair, the story was in the newspaper."

"And to be exact, it didn't mention me by name at all." Sara cocked her head with an insouciant smile.

"Sara, I think it's a …" Suddenly there was a crash of breaking glass from a second floor window in the Moore home. Sara and Johnny looked up as the front door opened and Bobby appeared.

The child was clearly upset, but he brightened when he saw his teacher. "Mrs. Goode!" He rushed down the front steps.

"Bobby, what's going on?" Another crash sounded from above, and this time they could hear a man yelling and cursing.

"Daddy's mad," Bobby said. "Mommy said she's coming to get me today, but Daddy doesn't like that." His chin quivered tightly. He was trying hard not to cry.

"Oh, Bobby," Sara took a few awkward steps forward, wondering if she should embrace the boy.

Before she could take another step, several assembled Lego sets sailed out the window above. Hitting the ground hard, they exploded into hundreds of individual bricks, blanketing the yard like confetti. Bobby ran over to the debris field and began gathering up the pieces.

Sara screamed, "No, Bobby!" and ran towards the boy. She was thrust aside by Johnny, who came from behind her. The sound of more breaking glass rang out, and Sara fell to her knees, dropping dog flyers as she used her hands to protect herself from incoming debris. She looked to Bobby just as Johnny threw himself on top of the boy, seconds before another volley flew out the window. Lego bricks and shards of glass rained down on Johnny. Fortunately, his jacket was thick enough to absorb most of the impact to his back, but his head was unprotected.

Bobby began to sob hysterically.

Sara stood up painfully, and shouted with every last bit of strength in her body. "David Moore! You stop that *right this minute*! Stop it!"

There was a moment of quiet, then David's sneering face appeared in the window.

"What the hell are you doing here?"

"What am *I* doing? What are *you* doing? You've hurt my friend. He was protecting Bobby from your temper tantrum. Now you need to calm down—!" She stopped herself short of saying "young man." David was behaving like one of her worst students, and she had gone into disciplinarian mode unwittingly.

David looked down and saw the heap that was Johnny and his son, Bobby. His sneer faded. His face was a blank mask.

Not knowing if she had pierced through David's rage and insanity, she knelt painfully next to Johnny. "Are you okay?"

At first, Johnny gave no reply, and Sara was alarmed to see bleeding gashes on the upper part of his body. Then she heard a faint groan as Johnny attempted to open his eyes.

"What?" He tried frame a question.

Sara stopped him. "Hush, Johnny." She gently rolled Johnny to his side and pulled Bobby out from under him. The sobbing boy fell into her arms. Sara struggled to hold Bobby and reach for the cell phone in her pocket. She dialed 911, a difficult task as she crying along with Bobby. She gave the call-taker the address and a brief description of the scene. Thankfully, Bobby seemed to have escaped any injury.

Bobby still burrowed in her arms, Sara ascertained that Johnny's breathing was even. He might be unconscious, but he was strong and would bounce back.

"Can I talk now?" Johnny's baritone caused her to jerk in surprise.

"Johnny! Oh, god, I'm so glad you're awake. I was so scared!" She hugged what she could reach—his arm—and held tightly.

"You told me to hush," Johnny said, "So I hushed." His voice was getting stronger, and he even had a note of humor despite his painful injuries.

The Brighton police, a fire truck and an ambulance pulled up in front of the Moore home. As emergency personnel fanned out across the lawn, Sara found herself supported to her feet. She told the sordid story of the blocks coming from the window and of David Moore's part in Johnny's injuries. She explained what Bobby had said, about his mother coming to get him and about David's unreasonable anger.

Johnny was attended by the medics, who assisted him onto a gurney, despite his protests, and moved him into the ambulance. Due to the copious bleeding of his head wounds, he was being taken to the local hospital.

"Stay with him," Johnny said, pointing to Bobby as he was lifted into the ambulance. Biting back sobs, she nodded. She wanted to go with Johnny, but she knew Bobby needed her more.

Many things happened at once. David Moore was led out in handcuffs. Johnny's ambulance left with its lights and sirens blazing. Bobby was taken into the custody of the police and a social worker until his mother could come for him. The fire engine moved out, as did the police, with David Moore and Bobby. Bobby had seemed frightened at first, but cheered when he was told maybe he could sound the siren later. Other unmarked vehicles came from the police department. Men in suits with cameras photographed the yard from every angle. Then they went upstairs, where Bobby's room had been ransacked by his father.

Sara answered questions when addressed, but tried to stay quiet and unobtrusive. She was in shock from what had just happened. It seemed almost like a dream, but the grass stains on her jeans and the soreness in her knees told a different story.

Oh, Johnny, she thought. He had unselfishly thrown himself in the path of disaster, saving Bobby...and keeping her from injury. He had followed his instincts and proved himself to be someone who would put himself in harm's way. Johnny had been the hero. He was more a hero than any superhero she could recall, and that included Batman.

Batman wasn't real, but Johnny was.

Last night, after receiving Adam West's note, Sara had acknowledged to herself that she wanted and needed a good man like Johnny. But today, Sara realized one more thing—she loved Johnny. She loved him with her heart and soul and every fiber of her being. If it took the rest of her life, she would let him know what he meant to her and would try to regain his respect and love. She'd been so blinded by her past that she hadn't left any room for Johnny to become a part of her present. That was about to change.

Sara's phone buzzed, showing Joe's name and number. She thumbed the answer button, "Joe?"

"Sara? Hi. Where are you?"

"Um. Joe. You're not going to believe this but I'm at David Moore's house. Well, actually sitting in front of it. Can you drive over and get me?"

"What? Are you kidding me? David Moore's house?"

"Joe, please just come. I'll explain everything when you get here." Sara almost ended the call, but then remembered an important detail. "Joe? Are you still there?'

"Yeah. Jen and I are walking back to your house."

"Joe, did anyone find Arf?" Sara crossed the fingers of her right hand.

"That's a good question, Sara. It was the reason I was calling you. Arf has been located."

"Oh, sweet lord, I can't believe it. Where was he found?" Sara could hardly breathe, she was filled with such relief.

"Funny thing. Char just called me asking where you were. She has Arf at her house."

"Char? But how?"

"Sara, Char found a family that wants to meet Arf. They're looking for a dog to adopt, and Char convinced them that Arf would be perfect for them. Anyway, she came over to your place last night to pick up Arf, but you weren't there. She noticed him in the back yard and decided to take him with her. I guess she didn't leave a note or anything, did she?"

"Leave a note? This is *Char* we're talking about, Joe. Not too keen on details. Listen, I need to hang up. See you soon, right?"

"Right-O."

Sara heaved a sigh of relief that Arf had been found. Then she dialed a new number. When Char answered the phone, Sara didn't allow her to get a word in edgewise. "Hello? Char? Listen, don't you dare give Arf away. He's my dog, and that's the final word on the subject. I want you to bring him to my house and put him right back where you found him. I'll be home in a little bit, but first I need to make a stop at the hospital. I'll call you back when I'm home, okay? Thanks."

Hanging up, no doubt leaving Char gaping and wondering what just happened, Sara stood up and stretched her arms to the sky. She was stiff, bone-tired and still a bit shaky, but her spirit was getting lighter with each passing moment. She was still worried about Johnny, and anxious to see him, of course, but she was filled with confidence that her hero—her...*boyfriend*?—would be all right.

After the chaos of the past few weeks, change was coming, turning chaos into a sweet semblance of order. Sara was prepared to face the future and embrace the good things: her friends, her family, her job, even Arf, and—yes—Johnny.

She wasn't a superhero. Heaven knew, spandex and a satin cape wouldn't make a good look for her. When all was said and done, she, Sara Goode, was a middle-aged school teacher, mutt-owner and Batman fan who still had a lot of living to do. She would give herself a chance with Johnny. And maybe in her future there would be another trip to a convention to see Adam West, where she would shake Mr. West's hand and, once again, tell him thanks.

END